THE MORTICIAN'S BIRTHDAY PARTY

Also by Peter Whalley

Harry Sommers' Novels

Robbers
Rogues
Crooks

THE MORTICIAN'S BIRTHDAY PARTY

Peter Whalley

Walker and Company
New York

Published in the United States of America in 1988 by the
Walker Publishing Company, Inc.

Library of Congress Cataloging-in-Publication Data

Whalley, Peter, 1946–
    The mortician's birthday party.

    Reprint. Originally published: London : Macmillan,
1983.
    I. Title.
PR6073.H35M6   1988   823'.914   88-75
ISBN 0-8027-1035-2

Printed in the United States of America

10 9 8 7 6 5 4 3 2 1

CHAPTER ONE

George Webster had been fascinated by human anatomy from an early age. Given a better education, he could probably have become a surgeon. It would, on the other hand, have been a poor joke had he ended up a butcher like his father.

As it was, a natural compromise between these two extremes, he was a mortician.

He was also, at the age of forty, suddenly and unexpectedly wealthy.

The *Arncaster Mirror* of November seventeenth 1978 explained it all. He had been left £67,000 in the will of Mrs Jean Lumbley, 'in recognition of the care freely given over many years'. A picture accompanying the article showed George smiling modestly.

It was his first appearance in the local press. But it would not be his last.

Mrs Lumbley, widowed, elderly and arthritic, had been his next-door neighbour. He had cleared her paths of snow in winter and leaves in autumn; had pruned her roses and cashed her old-age pension every Thursday; had even, though she was not to know it, arranged her hair and performed other little personal services for her after she had come into his professional care directly from the Women's Surgical Ward of Arncaster Royal Infirmary.

He had also attended the burial. Suspecting that there would be a poor turn-out, he had taken an hour off work and got a lift from the undertaker. To his surprise, ten or so relatives had materialized and were standing in a little, hopeful group around the open grave.

They were all outraged by the reading of the will, though none of them remained so long enough to contest it. George himself took the news of his good fortune calmly: he had surely deserved something somewhere along the way.

He knew immediately what he was going to do with the money, and that was to spend it. You could not take it with you. No-one could be more aware of that than George, whose normal day's work involved the processing of three to five corpses.

He was going to buy a big house and a big car. The car was easy: a Volvo Estate. The house took longer. In the end he allowed an estate agent to persuade him into buying the White House, a dilapidated monstrosity that was going for a song. It had nine bedrooms, servants' quarters and stables. The estate agent, who had had it on his books for seven years, was overjoyed. People who knew George put it down either to delusions of grandeur or to his morbid occupation having turned his head.

Within eighteen months he was married – to Elaine Ainsworth, some years his junior, whom he had met while on holiday. She had an air of superiority about her that suited the White House and the Volvo better than it did the natives of Arncaster.

'She knows what she wants anyway,' was among the more charitable of the views expressed. She settled into the large, dilapidated house as to the manner born and kept George working night and day to remedy in six months the more-or-less unbroken neglect of five hundred years.

The parties began before the house was even half-habitable. They took place most weekends and attracted quite a crowd, if only because so many were curious to see the inside of a building that had been a local landmark for so long. Not that the parties were occasions of much joy or wildness: more a rubbing of shoulders among the professional gentry of the town. They were gatherings for which George's status as mortician would have made him a questionable candidate had he not been the owner of the house – and, of course, the husband of the hostess.

It was shortly after one such party that Elaine disappeared. The news spread like wildfire: she had got her hands on a fair slice of George's inheritance and promptly scarpered. It seemed that she had gone about the town, withdrawing handfuls of cash – £1,500 from the Midland Bank, £2,000 from the Nationwide Building

6

Society, £2,000 from the Abbey National – and then taken the lot with her.

It would later be established that she had also, three days earlier, visited Armstrong's Jewellers with a Victorian pinchbeck bracelet for which they had given her £180 in cash.

'I know you can't force her to come back or anything,' George Webster told the police. 'But if you do hear anything about her then I'd like to know.'

They agreed that there was little for them to go on and filed her name under Missing Persons.

George hired a housekeeper to tend his rambling mansion and immersed himself in his work.

It was shortly afterwards that the naked body of a woman in her early thirties was washed ashore on a Devon beach. Casting around for an identity to attach to the mottled body, the police computer listed Elaine Webster (*née* Ainsworth) among twenty-nine other possibilities.

Which was the cue for George's second appearance in the *Arncaster Mirror*. 'Body That of Mortician's Wife?' was the headline. But by the following week's edition, the speculation was over. 'Body Not Wife of Local Man,' ran the headline. The article accompanying it went on to explain that a witness had appeared, a young man called Martyn James Culley, who had claimed to have met and talked to the missing Elaine Webster no more than two weeks earlier. When the pathologist's report stated that the Devonian corpse had been in the water for at least four weeks it became clear that, whoever it was, it was not Elaine.

An odd coincidence was that Culley himself had arrived in Arncaster only days earlier, had read the newspaper article and realized the significance of his chance meeting. He had gone himself to George Webster with the good news.

Whether out of gratitude or for some other reason, George Webster invited the young man to stay on at the White House where he lived for a few weeks as a sort of gardener and general factotum. This meant that he was still there when George gave his birthday party.

It was the first party, indeed the first social gathering of any

7

kind, that had taken place there since Elaine's abrupt departure. Most people saw it as George's attempt to demonstrate something – that he had survived his wife's desertion; that he was returning to the social whirl with or without her; or perhaps simply that even a mortician has birthdays.

Whatever the true reason, it was a party that was to guarantee his return to the pages of the *Arncaster Mirror*. This time he was given a banner headline across the middle of the front page: 'Tragic End To Birthday Party.'

There were several, slightly differing versions going the rounds of just what had happened at the birthday party but some facts were common to all: Elaine Webster was alive; she had been seen; she had turned up that evening; she had tried to kill George.

Some said that the police should have issued a warrant there and then for her arrest on the grounds of attempted murder instead of coyly stating, as they did, that she was 'wanted for questioning'. Others went further, saying that such a warrant should have been for the crime of murder since, one way or another, she had been directly responsible for George's death.

CHAPTER TWO

The only shelter available to Martyn Culley was a thin notice stating what was and what was not allowed on the motorway. He was standing at the bottom of the sliproad which formed Junction 18 on the M4 motorway. Although the date was May the fifth and it had therefore long been officially spring, it was raining heavily.

It had been raining when he had left his parents' house near Bristol. His mother had warned him that he would get wet. He had agreed nicely, kissed her on the forehead and sailed out with a promise to give her a ring when he got to where he was going. She would, he knew, have been delighted if the rain had forced him to stay, and would have been even more delighted if he had stayed there forever. But that would have been an admission of defeat far more difficult to face than any amount of rain.

His father had given him his usual lift to the motorway, had shaken hands briskly and left him. That had been two hours ago. He was now very wet indeed and not one jot nearer his destination.

A car stopped. Martyn sprang forward.

'Where're you going?'

The head sticking out of the passenger window was distinctly unappealing: a heavy stubble, unkempt hair, the butt of a cigarette between the lips. There was a readiness to laugh, or to turn nasty, about the face that suggested drink. Martyn instantly reviewed the possibilities: a drunken driver, speeding, accidents. . . . But the rain was running down his neck. He bent so as not to appear disrespectfully tall and put on an eager little smile.

'London.'

'Is that right?'

'Yes.'

'Well,' said stubble face, 'let's hope you get there then, eh.' And he laughed. There was more laughter from inside the car, which accelerated away up the sliproad.

Martyn slowly straightened up and went back to stand beside the sign. He settled down to wait again, less aware of the rain now that he had something to ponder on. What possible pleasure was there to be got out of raising the hopes of a soaking hitchhiker, and then dashing them in his face? Martyn had not thought to make a sign or shout anything after the car. He was so far from having any malice or ill-will in himself that meeting it in others only left him slightly shocked and puzzled.

He had come no nearer a real understanding when he saw that a Mini had stopped for him, its windows steamed up so that he was unable for a moment to see anyone inside. He hesitated, made wary by his recent experience, then approached in a little crouching run and opened the nearside door.

'London?'

His grateful smile made his answer superfluous. 'Please.'

'You'd better get in then.'

Again he hesitated. 'I'm a bit wet.'

'For goodness sake . . . !' she laughed. 'Get in!'

'Yes. Sorry. . . .' And he slid himself into the small seat, dropping his rucksack behind it.

'No use hitching and then telling people you're too wet to get in!'

'No. . . .' He shared her amusement at his absurd reaction.

'Have you been waiting long?'

It was the usual opening gambit and he responded eagerly, keen to show that he was willing to talk, to pay for his free trip with a little company which was, after all, why most of them stopped. He already felt protective towards her, grateful that she, a female alone, had taken the risk of picking up a lone male. She was attractive too. Small, neat features, mousey hair cut fashionably short and with an alertness about her that went with the Mini now bowling along at near seventy in the fast lane. He wanted to reassure her, show her that she had done the right thing in stopping for him. So he prattled on about himself.

'Well, philosophy mainly. I mean you had to do other things as well in your first year but then I majored in philosophy.'

She had asked him what he had studied at university. They had already established that he had been to Sussex, had left there three years ago and had had a succession of temporary jobs since.

'Probably wasn't a very good idea,' he went on. 'I mean looking back on it. As far as jobs are concerned, I suppose I should have done dentistry or accountancy or something.'

'I once studied psychology,' she said.

'Oh, that's different. . . .'

'I know! I know that's different.'

'Sorry,' he said, feeling foolish that he should have assumed that she would not. However, she seemed not to mind but rather to be amused. He felt very young beside her, though he would have only put her in her late twenties, no more than four or five years older than himself.

'What's your name?' she asked abruptly.

'Martyn,' he said. 'Martyn Culley.' And was wondering about adding, 'What's yours?' when she said, 'I'm Janet.'

'Janet.' He nodded.

'Janet Megson.' There was a moment's silence, then she repeated, 'Janet Megson.'

'Do you live in London?' he asked.

'No.' Another pause. 'Arncaster.'

'Arncaster,' he echoed with just a touch of surprise.

She turned quickly – anxiously? – and asked, 'Do you know it?'

'No, not er. . . .' He shook his head. His show of surprise had been perfunctory and would have been the same had she said Newcastle or Brighton or Wolverhampton; only now he had to find a reason for it. 'I have some friends who live there. A couple I knew at university.' Which was perfectly true – they were called Rob and Samantha and had both read English.

'But you've never been there?' she insisted.

'No.'

He wasn't even sure where Arncaster was. Somewhere in the north-west. Probably out beyond Manchester and Liverpool and the cotton towns. Was it, though, on the coast or simply near the

Lake District?

'You haven't got a northern accent,' he said.

'No, I haven't, have I,' was all that she replied. He feared for a moment that his observation had been misconstrued as criticism, till she went on: 'I come from Cirencester actually.'

'Ah.'

'Only I got married to a man from Arncaster. That was, what . . . three years ago. And so I went to live there.'

'I see.'

A sign at the side of the motorway indicated Hungerford. She asked him where he was going to in London and he told her of his friends in Hammersmith who were going to put him up while he went for his interview to be an air steward.

'A what . . . ?' she asked in surprise.

'Air steward. It's like a stewardess only . . . well, for men.'

Again she laughed at him, though without any unkindness. Not that he minded. It was a silly idea and one that he knew in his heart of hearts would come to nothing: he could no more see himself in an air steward's uniform than in that of a rear-admiral. But the interview in five days' time did at least give him a purpose in life and an excuse for going to London. He had, for the past three years since leaving university, been criss-crossing the country for the flimsiest of reasons – a friend's birthday, a pop concert, a cricket match. None of the reasons was important in itself but together they gave Martyn a life-style and an always-new destination.

'And do you think you'll get the job?' she asked him.

'No,' he said with a little laugh.

'Why not?'

'Well, not a lot to do with Philosophy, is it?'

'Not a lot,' she agreed.

'Although it would make a change,' he said. 'Instead of an in-flight movie, they could have me talking about Berkeley's theory of existence.'

'And what is Berkeley's theory of existence?'

He floundered for a moment at the unexpected question.

'Oh, er . . . it's that things only exist so long as they're seen. Once there's no-one there to see them then they stop existing.'

She gave a little smile, as though in recognition of something that was already familiar to her. 'Good old Berkeley,' she said. 'I think he's right.'

They went past Slough and already London was beginning.

'Are you still wet?' she asked.

'Oh, not much,' he lied, moving his neck against the damp collar of his denim shirt.

'Only we don't want you catching a cold.'

'Oh, don't worry,' he said. Then added truthfully, 'I don't think I've ever had a cold in my life.'

She glanced sideways at him.

'No, you look pretty fit. What do you do, football or swimming or what?'

The question embarrassed him. 'Well, I go running sometimes.'

'What, in those little running-shorts?'

There was, he felt sure, a suggestiveness about the question – and one that he felt bound to deflect.

'No, in a tracksuit.' And then immediately, 'What does your husband do?'

'Who?' She seemed genuinely surprised.

'Your husband.'

'Oh, him. I thought we were talking about your body.'

This time there was no mistaking the tease in her voice. Martyn gave a little laugh and found that he had clenched his hands. This hint of an approach from her made him uneasy. It was not that he found her unattractive; nor that this was the first time that such a thing had happened. He was, as his mother never tired of reminding him, a very pretty boy. Perhaps, more than anything else, his unease came from his continuing feeling of gratitude and his sense of responsibility towards her after she had picked him off the wet roadside. She should have been impressed by his pleasantness and courtesy, not by his long legs.

'Actually, my husband deals in bodies,' she said.

He gave a little grunt.

'But they don't run.' And she gave a rather silly laugh.

'Is he a doctor?' asked Martyn.

'No.'

13

She seemed to be waiting for more guesses so he tried, 'Chiropodist?'

'No.'

'A tailor?'

'No.'

'Well, something to do with physical education, then?'

'No, never mind,' she said, suddenly tiring of the game. 'Never mind what he is.'

It might have been two miles further on before she added, 'Whatever he is, it doesn't matter. What he can't see doesn't exist. Berkeley. Right?'

'Well, sort of,' said Martyn. He felt that he had rather undersold Berkeley's theory but knew that this was not the moment for a lecture on the subject.

They were coming to the A4 and Chiswick was signposted. The traffic bunched and slowed.

'Are you in a hurry?' she asked him.

'No,' he said, without thinking what she might mean. Anyway, you could hardly be a hitchhiker and in a hurry.

'Right,' she muttered. It seemed that she had come to a decision and began to concentrate purposefully on the driving.

They rose on the Chiswick flyover, then, breaking free from the traffic, were racing away in what seemed to Martyn to be the wrong direction.

Two minutes later they pulled up on the forecourt of a hotel. It was called The Mitre, displayed a two-star AA sign and advertised rooms and parking space. He knew now what was in her mind. What he was less sure of was his own reaction.

'Well,' she said.

'We seem to have stopped,' he said stupidly.

They were suddenly arch and awkward with one another. The journey that they had made together counted for nothing now that they were faced with the prospect of a greater intimacy.

'Oh, come on,' she said, opening the car door. 'Let's go and do it if we're going to.'

CHAPTER THREE

She had stopped to wait for him inside the revolving door, so close that he was almost thrown onto her.

'Listen,' she said. 'No ties, no hassle, just a nice friendly screw, then you go your way, I go mine, OK?'

'OK,' he said, and smiled reassuringly down at her.

'You do want to, don't you?' She seemed struck by genuine doubt.

'Yes!'

'Then don't look so worried!' And she went ahead of him to the reception desk.

He stood behind her, conscious of his damp, bedraggled appearance that went oddly with the determined gentility of the hotel. The carpeting was floral, the lighting subdued, the flowers by reception real. Martyn glanced behind him to see if he had left footprints.

She asked boldly for a double room and was asked if she preferred a double bed or two singles. A double, she said without consulting him, for which he was grateful. In fact, the cool, competent way in which she had taken on the whole of the transaction relieved him immensely. He remained standing behind her while she paid for the room in cash and then signed the book, apparently on behalf of both of them. He let his eyes rest on the hand-written lunch menu, reading and re-reading it down to where there was an unnecessary apostrophe in 'cheese's'.

'Twenty-one,' she said, passing him the key.

'Ah . . . yes.' He took it and looked at it intently as though suspecting a forgery.

'Come on, then,' she said brightly.

He caught up with her and they went together up a broad staircase.

They parted on the first landing to allow a man to pass by between them. He was in suit and tie and glanced in surprise at Martyn's jeans and trainers.

Martyn's own unease at this must have shown for, as they came together again, she caught his hand.

'Don't worry!' she hissed.

'I'm not,' he said, with a little laugh.

'Then stop frowning!'

He did. He was not, after all, going through any great crisis of conscience; just feeling scruffy and out-of-place. He was glad to get into the room with the door locked behind them.

The sex, when they came to it, was surprisingly good. Her brisk, no-nonsense approach, so effective in reception, was equally effective in getting them through the awkward business of coming to terms with the room, undressing and then coming together on the bed. 'You have that side,' she said, 'I'll have this,' and stepped out of her shoes while unbuttoning her jacket. He had to hurry not to be left behind. Once in the bed, their opening moves were restrained and polite until the passion that she had clearly been nursing along the motorway communicated itself to him and they began to race together easily and rhythmically towards satisfaction. Both of them were quiet about it and gave only the odd grunt or sigh of contented surprise. The bed did not creak. There was a compatibility between them that they might have talked for weeks and months without finding out what fornication had established in a little under five minutes.

For a little while afterwards it seemed that they were going to become friends.

'Thank you,' she said, withdrawing neatly to her side of the bed.

'My pleasure,' he said, and they shared a little laugh.

He was a considerate lover, by nature rather than from any deliberately practised technique, and always earned pleased compliments from his partners. His only failure had been in his second year at university with a highly-strung American post-graduate whose notions of love-making had bordered on the sadistic. She had pleaded that he should be rough and brutal with her, something he had been unable to do. 'Pathetic,' had been her final, considered opinion. Usually, though, his gentleness and sensitivity was a trade-mark that his partners afterwards remembered with affection.

He plumped up a pillow and leaned back against it. She did the same. A dressing-table faced them at the foot of the bed and it was through its mirror that they conversed.

'In case you were wondering,' she said, 'I don't do this with every hitchhiker that I pick up. In fact, you're the first.' Then, as honesty got the better of her: 'Well, the second. But only the second, I swear.'

'Well, it hasn't happened to me very often,' he replied, keeping the exchange light.

'I mean, why shouldn't we?' She was arguing with herself as much as anything. 'I'm never going to see you again, am I?'

'No,' he said. And then wondered.

'And I fancied you. I fancied you like anything. And it's not going to do anybody any harm, is it?'

'No.'

'Right.'

He sensed that she was still a touch dissatisfied with herself, as though in giving herself to him she had broken a resolution and been forced to recognize her own weakness.

'I'm sorry that you had to pay,' he said.

'Pay?'

'For the room.'

'It was my idea. Why shouldn't I pay?'

He gave a little shrug, not sure what the answer was. And, anyway, knowing that he had not enough money on him to really contest the fact.

'Unless you find it degrading,' she added.

It was difficult to tell from her distant image in the mirror whether or not she was teasing, but when he turned to her the little, mocking smile was clear.

'No,' he said, 'Just flattering.'

17

And they exchanged a chaste kiss, each catching a glimpse of themselves doing so in the mirror. And, at the same time, catching a glimpse of the other's glance towards it.

He had a shower in the small, adjoining bathroom while she got dressed. He came out from it with a towel wrapped round himself, knowing that he had a fine, broad physique and unable to resist the opportunity to display it for a moment.

She looked at him, then shook her head and tutted gently as though aware that something was wrong. He looked down at himself in surprise, not understanding her reaction.

'Oh, come on,' she said, and started to unbutton the blouse that she had just fastened. 'Let's have it again.'

He gave a little, pleased laugh.

'Might as well get our money's worth,' she said, and gave an apologetic smile. Again, for all her boldness, he had the impression of a woman who at least partly despised herself for this physical weakness of hers – this need to have it off with young men – and who might later have to pay for it in a fit of remorse. The idea, with its hint of vulnerability, attracted him even more to her and he took her head in his hands and kissed her gently before allowing her to complete her undressing.

Perhaps it was this edge of emotion that had come between them; anyway, the second copulation was less fun and more desperate than the first. She gave way to urgent little instructions which he hurried to obey, then reached her climax with a suddenness that almost spoiled his own. Even the bed had begun to creak.

'Well.' She sat up and cleared her throat. 'I've never done it twice like that before, and this time I do mean it.'

'Good,' he said simply.

'I think I'd better go,' she said without moving. 'I'm going to be late.'

'Late for what?' he asked.

He sensed that she was about to reply, then checked herself. 'Never you mind,' she said, and slid reluctantly from the bed. 'And, look, you needn't come.'

He did not understand her at first. 'Come where?'

'Well, I've paid for the room for the night. So you can stay if you want. Breakfast tomorrow morning as well.'

'Oh, yes,' he said, struck by the idea. The dual bout of sex had left him pleasantly tired; he could at least enjoy a snooze.

'In fact, you can have my breakfast as well,' she said, now swiftly repairing the damage to her face and hair in front of the dressing-table mirror.

He sat watching her, enjoying the novelty of the situation but with a faint, inescapable worry at the back of his mind that the cost – in every sense – of this little encounter was going to be borne entirely by her. For him it was an adventure, one for which he would be envied should he choose to boast about it – which he would not – and which he would certainly remember with relish. It did not seem fair that she might already be regretting it.

'Hey, and thanks,' he said.

'Thank you.'

'No, I mean . . . it's been really nice.'

'Yes,' was all she said, so that he was prompted to go further.

'You seem to be having second thoughts.'

'Do I?' She seemed surprised by the idea. Or surprised that he had noticed: he could not tell. 'No, not really. Just hope I haven't corrupted you for life, that's all.'

He felt put off by the joke, unable to pursue the matter further. She left five minutes later, exchanging goodbyes as they might have done had she simply been letting him out of the Mini after giving him no more than the lift which was all that he had been seeking.

He fell asleep and woke two hours later. The room was in darkness. For a moment he didn't know where he was, then remembered. There still seemed no hurry to be away, so he lay listening to the sounds of the traffic outside and the plumbing inside.

It seemed a shame that he was never to see her again. He had liked and even loved her for a little while and would have preferred to think that the experience might have been a beginning instead of an end. Her being that little bit older and more worldly than himself had been a new and attractive ingredient.

He knew where she lived of course. Arncaster. But to pursue her there would be a breach of trust that he had no intention of committing.

19

CHAPTER FOUR

A week later Martyn was standing at the bottom of the M1, holding a piece of cardboard on which he had written 'ARNCASTER' in capital letters.

He was one of a number of young hitchhikers out that morning who, following an unspoken rule-of-thumb, had spaced themselves some ten yards or so apart up the side of the sliproad. Two of them were girls and would doubtless be picked up first; otherwise it was a matter of smiling hopefully at any car or lorry that seemed to show an interest. But it was fine and he was in no hurry.

Needless to say, he had not been successful in his attempt to become an air steward. Indeed, the way that he had been addressed on his arrival at the British Airways offices as Matthew Culshaw instead of Martyn Culley had made him suspect that he had been called for interview by mistake, an impression that had been strengthened when he had been asked about his nursing qualifications. They had, though, given him his expenses and said that if he had not heard from them within a week then he could take it that he had not been successful. In fact, he knew the truth of his failure there and then as well as they did, but he had no wish to embarrass them and gave a dutiful performance in his role of the earnest interviewee before leaving the building with a sigh of relief.

Equally unsatisfactory had been the domestic arrangements in the house where he was staying. It was in Hammersmith: an address shared by between five and nine people – depending on the time of the year and the fluctuating fortunes of the nine, three of whom were actors and were frequently away working. When Martyn arrived they were all in rather crowded residence, the

20

central-heating had broken down and a bitter dispute had arisen as to the keeping of cats, which had to be fed and which kept fouling the kitchen floor.

The evening after his unsuccessful interview with British Airways, he was coming down the stairs from the room where space had been found for his sleeping-bag when the pay-phone in the hall rang and he answered it.

It was not for him – it was hardly likely that it would be – but for Jocelyn, one of the actors of the establishment. Asking the caller to wait, Martyn raced round in a vain search of the house.

'I'm ever so sorry,' he said, returning to the phone. 'I can't find him anywhere.'

'Oh well, never mind,' said the voice at the other end. 'I'll try again later.' And then added, 'Is that Martyn Culley, by any chance?'

'Yes,' said Martyn, surprised.

'Christ. It's Rob here. Rob Smithson.'

In that split second the idea of visiting Arncaster became a reality in Martyn's mind. Rob Smithson was the Rob of Rob and Samantha who had gone to live there. Martyn's sojourn in London was proving particularly unrewarding even by his undemanding standards. A quick departure might be a sensible solution. And where better than Arncaster for his next port of call?

'You must come and see us sometime,' urged Rob. 'We're only a few miles from the Lakes and can always fit you in somewhere.'

'All right,' said Martyn agreeably. 'Suppose I come next Monday?'

To which Rob, after only the slightest of pauses, agreed.

Having a bath that night, Martyn washed his hair and made himself face up to the truth of his own mixed motives. He was not, he had to admit, making the considerable journey in order to see Rob and Samantha, who were long-time acquaintances rather than close friends. Nor was he very interested in the Lakes, which he had seen at the age of seven and remembered as being bleak and inhospitable. And, all right, he was going to Arncaster because no-one at the moment was inviting him to go anywhere else and because he was in need of a new destination. But mostly he was

21

going because Janet Megson had said that she lived there.

It was unlikely, he knew, that he would see her, even if he were to spend several weeks in the place; even more unlikely that she would welcome it if he did. It was, after all, hardly fair to turn up on her doorstep and risk causing God-knew-what ructions. But he was not going to turn up on her doorstep. He had not the slightest idea where her doorstep was. He was going because it was her adopted town and he would like to see it. The remote possibility that he might see her again was not to be contemplated.

A lorry stopped and Martyn realized that it was waiting for him. He pulled himself up into a cab that was full of blaring pop music from a stereo cassette-player.

'Arncaster?' shouted the driver, a youngish man in a checked shirt.

'Yes, please,' Martyn shouted back.

'You're lucky then,' shouted the driver as he put the lorry back into gear. 'That's my next stop!'

'Great!' shouted Martyn.

It seemed a promising start.

CHAPTER FIVE

Arncaster mortuary was old, stone-flagged and permanently chilly, no matter what the weather outside. It was certainly an inhospitable place to be in the middle of a wet April. It was also quiet. George Webster's job as mortician there gave him plenty of time for contemplation. His customers were not talkative.

Nor indeed was either of his assistants. Maurice, nearing retirement and a Methodist lay-preacher, maintained a steady, respectful silence. Kevin, George's other assistant, was in his mid-twenties and might have been willing enough to talk had he had anything worth saying.

George arrived for work at nine o'clock, to find that the first corpse of the day had got there before him, delivered by ambulance after being declared dead in the Casualty Department of Arncaster Royal Infirmary.

'I used to know him,' said Kevin, who had been there to receive it. 'He used to teach me geography.'

'Police been yet?' asked George, who usually preferred to know as little as possible about the bodies to which he attended.

'The station called. Said somebody'd be down.'

In fact a police constable had at that moment appeared in the doorway. With the necessary witness now present, they were able to go to work, taking the body from its refrigerated compartment and undressing it.

'He's called Mulroon,' said Kevin helpfully.

'You know him, do you?' said the policeman.

'He used to teach me geography.'

'Well, you'd think he'd know better than to go driving into

23

lampposts then,' said the policeman, filling in the accident form.

George ignored the joke. He had long observed that visitors to the mortuary and its routine processing of death often reacted with jocularity, as if to hold the whole business at arm's length.

After taking off the clothing, they emptied the pockets, finding a motley collection of wallet, loose change, credit card, pens, handkerchief and Polo mints – all of which the police constable collected together and took with him as he left to inform Mrs Mulroon of her husband's death.

'Let's have him in the Chapel then,' said George, yawning.

He had gone to bed late and slept badly, spending much of the night lying awake beside the hunched body of his wife who, as always, was turned away from him, keeping fastidiously to her own side of the bed.

The police constable returned with a distressed Mrs Mulroon. The Chapel into which she was shown was windowless and bleak, brightened only by the sprays of flowers, the superfluous offerings of other people's funerals that the undertakers were in the helpful habit of leaving there. Like the rest of the building, the Chapel had the feeling of being underground. Its curving roof with supporting pillars seemed designed to hold great weights. It was always a small surprise to people when they stepped outside again and found themselves at ground level.

Mr Mulroon, beyond caring about such architectural peculiarities, lay on a trolley, the worst effects of the car crash hidden by a spotless shroud.

'Is this your husband?' asked the constable formally.

'Yes,' said the woman, and burst into a flood of tears.

This meant, since the death had been as a result of an accident, that a post mortem would have to be held. The Coroner's permission was obtained and George telephoned to inform Mr Charlesworth, one of the two pathologists who served the area.

'Be with you in an hour,' he said.

This gave George the chance to send Kevin out for a sandwich – there had, of course, been no question of Elaine preparing any breakfast that morning – and to retire to his small office, the only room in the mortuary where he could smoke.

He tried reading the copy of the *Sun* that he had collected, as usual, on his way to work, but he could not seem to concentrate. The previous night's row with Elaine had been their most violent yet and had left him with a dark sense of despair that made it impossible to forget, even for a few moments.

They had been in the large kitchen of the White House, a room whose original architecture was not, in fact, unlike that of the mortuary. He had eaten without complaint the fish fingers and chips that she had thrown at him but, instead of leaving him to it as was her wont these days, she had started to natter and nag about jobs that needed doing. He had defended himself, pointing out that he was working all day while she was at home. The exchange had escalated and become dangerous.

By the time he had finished his meagre dinner, the topic of the jobs that needed doing had been left far behind.

'Why do you despise me?' he had yelled. 'You don't even bloody well talk to me properly anymore!'

'No,' she had replied coolly. 'But then, what the hell have we got to talk about?'

'Nothing!'

'Exactly.'

It was the truth of the observation that made it unforgiveable.

'So why do you stay for God's sake?' he went on, knowing himself to be unwise. 'Why stay if we can't even talk to one another?'

She had seemed to consider the question, then gave a small shrug. 'I don't know. Why do *you* stay? Let's face it, we're both stuck in a marriage that neither of us wants!'

This was the first time it had actually been said; even if both of them separately knew the truth of it already.

'You rotten bitch!' He had been trembling and on the verge of striking her but then, knowing even in his anger that that would give her the upper hand forever, he had instead picked up his coffee-cup and hurled it across the kitchen. It had hit the Aga cooker and bounced off without breaking – which had made her laugh.

'I'll kill you,' he had said in tearful despair and, despite his

25

resolution not to touch her, had grabbed her by the shoulders. She had frozen, making no move to escape or to oppose him. Just waited, staring at him. He would never – her eyes told him – dare to hurt her in the way that he yearned to.

'Rotten bitch!' he had said again, and pushed her away.

She had allowed herself to follow his push, exaggerating its force, and hit her head against the wall.

'I see,' she said, with a little, triumphant smile. 'You're going to beat me up now, are you?'

He had sworn at her, using obscenities that were foreign to him but that, even so, now seemed feeble and incapable of conveying the passion that he felt.

'You're a creep,' she had said when he had finished. It was a considered, serious judgement. His use of physical force had removed all inhibitions between them. 'You want to stick to your dead bodies. I'm sure you're much more at home with them.' She had gone to the door, then turned for a final riposte. 'And don't touch me ever again. Not ever again.'

He should not, he knew, have allowed her to see the extent of his hopelessness. Now there would be no going back, not even to the cold but polite war which had been the reality of their marriage for the past year.

He stayed up late, drinking whisky and wandering around the huge, silent house. At one point, glass in hand, he had gone out into the still largely overgrown gardens and walked round the site where they had planned to have the swimming-pool, and the paddock, knee-high in grass, which Elaine had thought might one day have been turned into a tennis court. All of it, with the white-walled house picked out in the moonlight, now seemed a gigantic folly, a monument to his stupidity and ambition. He had been content as a bachelor mortician in his small, semi-detached bungalow – not happy exactly, no, but with no cause for the kind of grief which he now felt. That was before Mrs Lumbley had bestowed her fortune upon him – and now even that good-hearted woman came in for a share of his curses – and given him the scope to indulge his arrogant fancy that he, George Webster, might be as other men and have a fine house and fine wife to go with it.

Kevin stuck his head round the door.

'D'you want to start on that P.M? Mr Charlesworth'll be here in twenty minutes.'

'Yes.' George sighed and got to his feet. 'I'm coming.'

They slid the body from its drawer and wheeled it into the dissecting-room. A place designed for the dismantling of the human body; a caricature of an operating-theatre with its long, scrubbed tables and the gulleys below to carry away the blood.

'Right,' said George. 'Lift him on.'

Though the final responsibility for any post mortem would always rest with the pathologist, it was the mortician and his assistants who did the donkey-work. The body had to be dissected and its organs laid out for inspection before the pathologist, the star of the show, would come sailing in, have a poke and prod around and deliver his verdict; leaving them to fit all the bits together again.

Still, it was a relief for George to be working and to have his mind taken off his wife and his house and the whole bloody mess that his own life had become.

Kevin wrote the name 'Dennis Mulroon' and his age 'forty-one' on the board at the head of the dissection table while George took a knife and opened the body from the top of the sternum, past the umbilical to the pubis. Then he cut a neat V-shape round the neck so that the skin could be opened like the two halves of a waistcoat.

'It's funny seeing him like this after he taught me geography,' observed Kevin.

George took out the throat, tonsils, adenoids and thorax, the lungs and the heart, then the liver and, with it, the gall bladder. He set all of them alongside the body in their respective relationships to one another.

'No gall-stones,' he muttered, feeling for them out of habit.

Then out came eighteen feet of small intestine and the large ascending colon; which, being less easy to arrange neatly on the table, went into a basin.

As did the stomach and its contents, which came next.

Then the kidneys, right and left, and the spleen from its place just behind the left kidney.

27

Kevin stood and watched, slightly resentful that he was allowed to do so little. George, who still found pride and pleasure in his job, was always reluctant to break off and let someone else complete it.

He moved back up to the head, cutting the skin from the crown to the back of each ear so that he could pull the scalp apart and get at the skull. Anticipating this, Kevin held the necropsy saw ready, switched it on and passed it over. The circular blade vibrated and buzzed, throwing up a fine mist of bone. Finally, the top of the skull – now looking, as Mr Witzman, the previous pathologist had often observed, like a white bone version of the yarmulka, the Jewish prayer-cap – was lifted off and the brain exposed.

The door opened as Mr Charlesworth arrived.

'Morning,' he sang out.

'Ready for you in just one minute,' said George, concentrating.

'Oh don't worry,' said Mr Charlesworth, crossing to where the gowns and wellingtons were kept. 'I'm not in a hurry. And I'm sure he isn't.'

George had cut away the protective membrane of the dura and pulled back the brain to expose the criss-cross of the optic nerves. He cut through these, then the pituitary gland, then the spinal process nerves. So that, as Mr Charlesworth approached the table, snapping on his rubber gloves, he could lift out the brain and the cerebellum and place them by the side of the head on the dissecting-table.

'Dear me, what happened to him?' asked Mr Charlesworth, seeing the bruised and cut body.

'Drove into a lamppost,' muttered George, stepping back now that the first part of his task was complete. He motioned Kevin forward, happy to let him take over now that it was a matter of merely assisting while the pathologist did his work. His secret view of his own role was that it complemented that of the pathologist. He was not an assistant or a subordinate; rather a specialist in a slightly different but related field.

It was the importance of his work that he had never been able to make Elaine understand – or rather that she had never been willing even to contemplate. For many months after they were married she had simply side-stepped any attempt by him to talk about it.

28

He had eventually challenged her: 'Don't you want to know anything about it?'

'No, I don't, thank you very much,' she had retorted tartly.

'It takes years of experience and study, you know,' he had urged weakly. 'It's not everybody who can do it.'

'I'm sure it isn't.'

And he had had reluctantly to accept the fact that the two areas of his life – his work and his home – would henceforth remain apart.

Only now did he see it as the first step in a process that would end with him the despised and barely-tolerated husband of a wife whose social aspirations were apparently endless and for which he would have to slave night and day.

Kevin was now replacing the brain and cerebellum from which Mr Charlesworth had cut small samples. All the organs had been weighed and the weights recorded on the board in Kevin's spidery handwriting.

Mr Charlesworth, singing quietly to himself, was examining the contents of the stomach. He would then move on to the intestines, spleen, rectum and bladder, taking samples and transferring them into specimen bottles and jars.

Even though the immediate cause of death – collision with a lamppost – was indisputable, the State wisely insisted that Mr Charlesworth should search for evidence of drugs, alcohol, poison, heart attack, stroke or any other physical condition that might have been the true cause of the accident. Who was to say that Mrs Mulroon, poor woman, had not been secretly and systematically poisoning her husband? Unlikely perhaps, but the law could only operate on the cynical assumption that even the most innocent-looking of deaths might be masking what was, in fact, murder.

He thought again of Elaine. Why had she ever married him? It was a question with which he increasingly tormented himself. Indeed, he had put it to her that morning when, as he was leaving for work, she had come down the staircase, still in her nightdress.

'If everything you said last night was true. . . .' he began.

'It was.'

'Then why the hell did you ever marry me?'

She had stopped where she was, above him, no doubt conscious of the dramatic setting that the wide, oak staircase gave her.

'I just wanted to get married, that was all. I thought it wouldn't matter who to.'

It was an answer designed to insult rather than to inform, but there was probably some truth in it. Probably equally true was that she had been attracted by the prospect of his money, and by being mistress of his house. Perhaps she hadn't understood her own motives at the time: had simply felt herself pressured into marrying him and now bitterly regretted it. Not that he cared. He was past being fair, past trying to understand and make allowances. She had made him more miserable and wretched than he had ever thought it possible to be, and he hated her for it.

Mr Charlesworth lifted the left leg of the corpse and squeezed in order to coax the twenty mls of blood that he needed from the femoral artery. Once this was achieved, he added a drop of citrate solution to stop clotting and filled the two containers that would go for analysis.

'Right,' he said, peeling off his rubber gloves. 'I think that about does it.'

George snapped out of his reverie and moved forward to take from Kevin the task of reconstituting the body so that it could later be viewed with equanimity by relatives and friends. Not that everything was going back in quite the way that it came out. The organs were piled without ceremony into a plastic bag and replaced *en masse*. The neck was padded up with wet cotton wool and the top of the skull slotted back on without much of the brain that it had originally protected. Then, George starting from the top and Kevin from the bottom, they stitched up the incisions that George had begun making.

Meanwhile, Mr Charlesworth was taking off his gown and wellingtons and talking into his cassette-recorder: '. . . Death was, in my opinion, caused by multiple injuries, consistent with a head-on collision. Five of the ribs were broken and had penetrated both lungs. Bleeding from which had entered the chest cavity. The neck had also been broken. . . .'

The stitching-up completed, George and Kevin began washing and drying the body and combing and setting the hair, doing both with a carefulness that belied the assault they had been so recently making on it.

'Bye bye,' called Mr Charlesworth, striding out and leaving the door to crash to behind him.

Once its toilet was complete, they lifted the body onto a trolley and fitted a shroud over it. At last, gutted within and respectable without, it was ready to be returned to its refrigerated compartment for a well-earned rest.

From start to finish the post mortem had taken something over an hour and a quarter.

'Can I go for my break now?' asked Kevin, who, unlike George, preferred to get out of the mortuary when he could.

'Yes,' said George. 'I'll have 'em give you a shout if anything else turns up.'

Left alone, he rang the Coroner and informed him, as was his duty, that the post mortem had been completed. The Coroner thanked him and said that he would inform the appropriate funeral directors that the body was now available to them.

George returned to his office and meticulously recorded the details of that morning's work. Life, after all, had to go on, even if he could not help feeling that his own had little point or purpose left to it.

The only tiny consolation that he could find was that, since Elaine would clearly be indifferent as to when he returned home that evening, he could now definitely go and see Josie again. That is, go to the cheap restaurant where she worked and hope that she would again serve him and that he could again get talking to her.

God knew, he was hardly the type to go picking up waitresses – even if Josie did seem the type of waitress who might enjoy being picked up. Would she even remember him? At least she did not seem the type to patronise or tease. She seemed refreshingly straightforward; the sort of girl who would say what she felt.

And what she had said had been, 'I'm sick of this place, I am. I'd do anything to get out of it,' while, he could have sworn, looking him straight in the eye.

At that time, two nights ago, he had been his usual self. He had

31

smiled weakly in agreement and let the matter drop. Now, as he struggled against his ruined marriage and his monstrous, ever-demanding house, she alone seemed to offer a remote prospect of solace and comfort.

CHAPTER SIX

Coming off duty at half-past-five, George strolled through the narrow, Victorian streets of the town, still without having shaken off his burden of despair. It had been a quiet day with only one other post mortem in the middle of the afternoon – the victim of a heart attack, found slumped in his seat at the Hippodrome, the town's cinema, before the main film had even begun.

George had left his car at the mortuary so that he might have this walk in the fresh air and it now revived him a little; as did the feeling of a town going about its business; with people rushing to catch shops before they closed or buses before they left. He began to lose his earlier conviction that everything was sour and worthless.

The restaurant towards which he was heading, the Friar Tuck, was the only one in Arncaster that was not Indian or Chinese or fast food. The menu in the window had faded so as to be almost illegible, except for the prices which were handwritten in as they increased. Inside, there were murals of the Lake District and an illuminated tank of exotic fish, one of which was dead. George settled himself at a corner table, disappointed that there seemed to be no sign of Josie. 'Damn,' he said to himself: it seemed unfair that even this small consolation should be denied him.

Then, suddenly, there she was, swinging her way through the tables towards him, carrying a grubby menu.

'Hello,' he said and smiled up at her.

It was a moment before she recognized him.

'Oh hello,' she said, and gave a quick, minimal smile. The affability that she had shown on their earlier meeting had vanished.

33

Perhaps her life, too, had its share of troubles.

'And what have you got today then?' he asked, taking the menu.

'Same as last time.'

He ordered scampi, instinctively avoiding the liver and kidneys that were the menu's only meat dishes.

'By the way,' he said quickly before she could move away, 'What time do you finish here tonight?'

Her expression hardened. She was no doubt tired of being chatted up by customers.

'Why?'

'I wondered if you wanted to come for a drink, that was all,' he said, glancing to see that no-one else in the place could overhear him.

'With you?'

He did not resent the impertinence of her reply. It was no more than he had expected.

'Last time I was in', he said, 'you sounded as though you might be looking for another job.'

A flicker of interest came and went in her face. 'Might be.'

'I might be able to help you, then,' said George. He was amazed at his own audacity. How could he help her? Suppose that she were to accept, to say that she would come, what was this help that he would then offer? It was only the hopelessness of his marriage that was making him so reckless outside it.

'All right,' she said. 'I finish at half-seven.' And, hips rotating, she tracked back between the tables to the kitchens. His eyes followed her and he was too late to hide his stare when she turned quickly at the kitchen door and glanced back. She was frowning slightly as if she could not be sure of what was going on.

Ten minutes later she was back with the scampi.

'I'll pick you up outside then, shall I?' he said.

She shrugged. 'Yeah. OK.'

'I'll be in a white Volvo estate.'

Another shrug. White Volvo estates were, in her considered opinion, nothing to write home about.

He began to eat. At least he still had his money, or anyway enough of it for the financial side of his life not to be a problem.

Despite all of Elaine's grandiose ambitions there was still over £15,000 left in the kitty. For all her hard-faced posing, Josie seemed the kind of straightforward girl to whom that kind of simple fact might mean a great deal.

He made an early escape from the restaurant, fearing that to linger over his meal would give her the opportunity to change her mind. She watched him go without comment, then went to clear the table that he had left.

He stopped in the flagged square in the centre of town, bought an evening paper and sat on a bench to digest his meal while the town hall clock crept its way round to seven-thirty. There were few people about. It was that period of peace between the ending of the day and the beginning of the night; and for a moment it inclined him towards a more optimistic view of his life. Perhaps his only real mistake had been to stake everything on his marriage. Coming late to it, he had expected too much from it. Elaine and he would surely, as things went on, find a less painful way of living together; they would settle for something less than the idyllic vision with which they – or at least he – had begun. He would continue to work on the house and its grounds, would go daily to the mortuary and would – touch wood – occasionally permit himself an evening out with Josie, just to add a little spice to the proceedings.

The excitement that he now felt at his planned rendezvous with this young girl – how old was she anyway? eighteen? nineteen? – was one that, ironically, reminded him of his feelings during the two weeks in Torquay during which he had met and courted his wife.

They had both been staying at the Hotel Juno, set high above the seafront and had got talking on their third night there as they stood next to one another at the bar.

'Been a lovely day, hasn't it,' she had said.

'Yes,' he had agreed abruptly, taken by surprise, then regretted that he had not offered to buy her a drink and thus been able to continue the conversation.

The following night he lingered in the lounge until he saw her enter and was thus able to ensure that they again arrived together at the bar. His offer of a drink was accepted, they talked about one thing and another and it was she who suggested that, since they both seemed to be alone, they might as well share a table for dinner.

By the end of the meal he was head-over-heels in love with her. She was attractive, some fifteen years younger than himself and had an educated, worldly air about her. He was happy to think of her as his social superior: his capture of her would then be that much more of a conquest. (He had not, of course, suspected then that she would one day share this view of their inequality and treat himself and his work with such undisguised contempt.)

She told him that she was called Elaine Ainsworth, came from Cirencester, was unmarried and had come away alone to recuperate after having been ill for some weeks with glandular fever. He told her of his unexpected legacy from Mrs Lumbley and of the White House.

Two days later they went together on a coach excursion to Plymouth and walked along the Hoe in the spring sunshine.

'I haven't told you what my job is, have I,' he said. It had already been established that she was a librarian but was disillusioned by the tediousness of much of the work.

'No,' she said.

'Only it's not one that everybody likes the sound of.' She looked at him in surprise and waited. 'I'm a mortician.'

'How unusual,' she said, and he was relieved to see that she was smiling.

Most days after that they spent together until, all too quickly, it was their last night. Forsaking the hotel, they ventured out to an Italian restaurant where the wine and the comfortable feeling of Miss Lumbley's legacy had emboldened him to wonder aloud whether their relationship might have some future beyond their holiday fortnight. She admitted that she too had wondered whether it might. They had gone on to talk about the White House; although Elaine had, of course, never seen it, she seemed to have quickly grasped its potential and was full of ideas for possible improvements and modernizations.

They walked back along the promenade. The tide was in and, leaning over the rail to gaze at it, they might have been on the deck of a ship.

36

'Will you marry me?' he asked, without being aware of having made any conscious decision to do so.

She made one trip north to see her future home before the wedding. He met her at the station, then drove with deliberate slowness up the steep hill that rose for nearly a mile from the edge of town before the house appeared at its summit. By this time he had paid builders and plumbers and specialists in damp-proofing to put right the worst features of the house's neglect, but, even so, his observant lover's eyes had noticed the look of surprise and dismay that came over Elaine's face before she was able to hide it and become enthusiastic.

There was, admittedly, still much to be done. The white walls of the house were overlaid with dirt and moss; the garden had become a wilderness; there was even the odd broken window still visible on the top floor. Her confidence returned, however, as they walked round and he pointed out to her the scope that the house offered and swore that he would work night and day to see it realised.

Two weeks later, they were married in a small church in Cirencester. The service was High Anglican and, on Elaine's insistence, everyone was in formal dress.

As they came out of the church, the sun came out from behind the clouds that had earlier threatened rain. The photographer marshalled them into a group, someone threw some confetti and people passing in the road beyond the railings paused to look in at them.

At that moment, standing there among the gravestones with his bride on his arm, he had been supremely happy.

His new sister-in-law, Margaret, came up and gave him a little kiss. 'Look after her, won't you,' she said.

'I will,' he promised with a smile. 'I'll see she has everything she ever wanted.' At the time it had been a serious statement of intent.

The town hall clock struck a quarter past seven. George folded up his newspaper and dropped it into a waste-bin. It would not do to be late.

He picked up his car from outside the mortuary, calling in first to check with Maurice that everything was as it should be.

'Yes,' said Maurice, 'so far as I'm aware. You off out for the night?'

'Yes,' said George, without elaborating. Then he asked, 'Elaine hasn't called, has she?'

Maurice shook his head. George wished him good night and left, not sure how pleased he was that his wife had not called. It certainly confirmed her indifference as to whether he arrived home or not – and therefore helped him justify to himself the date with Josie – but was that really what he wanted?

She was fifteen minutes late coming out of the restaurant. He thought for a moment that she had not seen him and was going straight past but then suddenly she was trying the car door and he had to hurry to lean across and unlock it so that she could climb in. The black dress had been swopped for jeans and a sweater which made her look younger and more vulnerable. He could not help reflecting on what an odd couple they made and wondered for the first time what people who saw them might think.

'Well,' she said, glancing round at the interior of the car, 'where're we going then?'

'Have you eaten?' asked George. He had thought of one or two places to which they might go and run little risk of being spotted.

'Course I have!' she said with a little grimace of contempt. 'Least they can do, isn't it, seeing as it's supposed to be a café!'

'Ah yes, of course,' admitted George. He would have to think again. 'Do you know The Leather Bottle?'

'No,' she said. 'Surprise me.'

And off they went. Leaving the town behind them until its tree-lined outskirts turned into the real countryside. He drove faster than usual, feeling an absurd need to display some sort of dash in front of her.

'So what's the job then?' she said, lighting a cigarette.

He knew, of course, that she would ask, and that, in truth, he had no job to offer either to her or to anybody else. All he did have was a vague notion that he might offer to lend her money if she showed any inclination to set herself up in her own small shop or café.

'Wait till we get there,' he said. 'No rush is there?'

She gave a little, indifferent grunt and settled down to watch the

38

passing scenery through half-closed eyes.

The Leather Bottle was a pub of some genuine antiquity standing on the banks of the canal. George had thought of it on the spur of the moment without knowing why. Now it occurred to him that Elaine had mentioned it as somewhere that she had visited and found interesting. It was a popular stopping-point for boats and there were several there, tied up on both banks.

George and Josie sat at a wooden table outside. He brought her the rum and coke that she asked for and, anxious to delay further the question of jobs, asked her to tell him about herself.

She did so without any reluctance or self-consciousness.

'I was in a probation hostel up to four months ago,' she said, as if this were nothing out of the ordinary. 'Then they let me out when I got the chance of this job on account of there's accomodation goes with it, see? So 'course I can't leave it without I get another job that has accommodation as well. Or else they can take me back inside.'

'Difficult,' muttered George. He saw now why she had been so easily persuaded to come with him. Her suggestion of a criminal past made him nervous. Might he not be getting himself into deep water? Looking only for consolation after the hostility shown by his wife, was he not in danger of getting involved not only with a young girl (how old was she anyway for God's sake?) but with her probation officer as well?

'Are you married?' she said, sounding as if she did not much care one way or the other.

He cleared his throat. 'Yes. Yes, sort of.'

She nodded. 'They usually are. And what sort of business are you in then?'

'Medical,' he said vaguely. It was the nearest he had ever come to lying about his job and was another pinprick of warning that this situation might have complications far beyond those he had envisaged.

'You're not a doctor, are you?' she said, looking at him with a new curiosity.

'No,' he said. 'I'm on the, er, the administrative side.' Which completed the lie.

'So what's the job for me in that then?' she said. 'I hope you don't

39

think I'm going to be a nurse or anything!' And she gave a sudden hee-haw of a laugh that made one or two people on nearby tables look round.

'No, no,' he said quickly. 'No, I'm sort of in business as well.' Then, seeing as her glass was nearly empty, 'Can I get you another one?'

She agreed that he could and he hurried away to the bar. Waiting to be served, the unchivalrous thought struck him that he could easily slip out by another door, jump into his car and desert her there and then; except that he would then live in fear for weeks to come that he would bump into her and be recognised. There was no knowing the kind of scene there might be. She might even assault him. Her background of unspecified criminality frightened him.

So he went back out with the drink, resolving to bring the charade to a quick and bloodless end. The whole idea had been a foolish mistake from the start. Perhaps he could pretend to offer her some totally unsuitable job, let her turn it down, then drive her home – cut his losses before anything could get out of hand.

As he arrived at the table, where Josie had meanwhile lit another cigarette and successfully outstared the curious glances that she had been getting from the next table, a man and a woman were coming out of one of the canal boats that were tied up on the opposite bank.

'I'll walk you to your car,' said the man, his voice carrying across the water.

'Have they got any crisps?' said Josie to George. 'Then we could feed the ducks.'

But George's attention had been wrenched away by the woman's reply which came floating over to them.

'If you like,' she was saying. 'See that I don't get raped or something.' And then a little laugh that he, George, knew only too well.

'I said have they got any crisps?' repeated Josie.

But George was staring across at Elaine as she slipped her arm through that of the man from the canal boat and they began to walk away together.

He felt a savage sense of fury and humiliation but mixed with it was a fear, a warning voice, that kept him quiet and still. Then, suddenly, it was the fear that leaped into prominence over all else as Elaine said, 'Oh, wait . . .' as if remembering something and turned to go back to the boat. In a moment of pure anguish for George, they faced one another, man and wife, across the canal.

She saw him with Josie, saw what he was doing there, saw everything.

He only saw her lips move, forming the one, astonished word, 'Christ . . . !' as the man from the canal boat looked at her in surprise.

'Is there something the matter?' asked Josie.

CHAPTER SEVEN

'She was obviously a slut.'

'You don't know her,' George defended weakly.

'I don't have to know her. I could see she was a slut.'

'And what about you?'

'Well, what about me?' and, as George hesitated: 'What about me? You're going to compare me with your slut? And, anyway, how old was she? Sixteen? You checked that she's sixteen, did you? I mean I wouldn't want you to be in trouble with the law!'

They were back home that same night. Elaine had been waiting for him the moment he had walked through the door after hastily depositing Josie back in town. The confrontation had begun in the hallway, then transferred to the sitting-room. Elaine was standing; George sitting.

'I've only ever seen her once before,' he insisted for what felt like the tenth time. 'And we were only having a drink.'

'You enjoy one another's conversation, is that it?'

'Anyway,' he attempted to counter-attack, 'what were you doing that gives you the right to criticise me? What were you doing on that boat with that . . . that . . .'

'Gordon.'

'Yes. All right, Gordon. What were you doing with him?'

She gave a composed little smile, looked him straight in the face and said, 'I'd been to visit him. He's a friend of mine. I'd also been to visit his wife, who is also a friend of mine.'

'His wife?'

'Yes.'

He gave a snort of disbelief. 'I didn't see any wife there!'

'No, you wouldn't,' said Elaine calmly. 'But she was. She was inside the boat; which, of course, was why you didn't see her.'

He was sure that it was a lie. What was even more insulting, he got the distinct impression that she did not really care whether he thought it a lie or not. Her contempt for him was such that even the alibis for her adultery were tossed off without much thought or attempt to really convince him.

'I didn't see any wife there,' he repeated.

'No, of course not, you stupid man! His wife was inside the boat! Understand? She was inside and that was why you couldn't see her!'

'Prove it.'

She smiled at the feeble counter. 'I don't need to prove anything.' Which was true. 'Whereas you – you didn't care who saw you and your little slut, did you? You were there for all the world to see, weren't you! The little girl with her sugar daddy!'

Her voice had risen so that she was practically shouting. And not so much in anger as in triumph. She was enjoying the whole thing. His brief, foolish flirtation with Josie had given her a blank cheque as far as their lives together were concerned.

'I'm not her sugar daddy!' he protested.

'Oh no? It's an affair of the heart, is it?' The sarcasm was almost tangible. 'Moonlight and roses and dirty weekends!'

He sighed and gave up. She would believe what she chose, and she chose to believe that he was guilty.

This added a cruel feeling of injustice to everything else he had suffered that night. After the awful shock of seeing her on the other bank of the canal, there had been the embarrassing business of getting rid of Josie and then his return to the house. He had been in a desperate state of mind, convinced that Elaine was about to declare her love for another – Gordon or whatever his name was – and inform him that their marriage was over. But no. Instead, the evening had given her a new authority over him and one which she showed every sign of exercising with gusto.

'Look,' he tried for a last compromise, 'Why don't we just say that we've both been a bit silly and leave it at that? Eh? Forget all about it and . . . well, and start again?'

She actually laughed aloud at the proposition.

'Please,' he begged. 'For the sake of our marriage.'

'You should have thought of that before you picked up your slut.' .

He sighed. 'I know. I'm sorry.'

'And don't worry about our marriage.'

He waited. Here now was the price that he was going to have to pay.

'I mean I'm not going to ask for a divorce or anything. Why should I? I've got everything I want. I've got this house. I've got the money. I'm not going to settle for just part of it. Why should I when I've got the lot? No, dear, don't worry. No divorce. We'll just carry on as we are.'

It was the modus vivendi that he had hoped they would in time achieve, but this was entirely on her terms.

'So you're going to go on seeing Gordon?' he challenged.

'I'll go on seeing who I want,' she replied, unruffled. 'It won't be any concern of yours.'

'Thank you,' he said, defeated.

'Now,' she said, 'I'm going up to bed. I think you'd better sleep in the spare room, don't you?'

He did not argue and she left the room with the air of one who considered everything settled to her satisfaction.

'I could kill you for this,' he muttered. It was an expression of pure frustration and meant nothing.

He rose from his chair and, opening the french windows, went out into the garden. A chilly wind surprised him, plucking at his hair and making a low moan amid the trees and bushes.

He knew that he could not stand up to her. From the start he had willingly subordinated his wishes to hers, first out of love, then out of necessity, to avoid the rows and the nagging that were provoked by any attempt to oppose her. Was it she who had changed? Had she been transformed by his wealth and that dismal, echoing house on their lonely hill? Or had she been a monster from that first, fateful meeting in Torquay, and had he, inexperienced as he was, been blinded by infatuation?

More importantly, what could he now do about it? The idea of divorce frightened him, particularly given her stated intention of opposing it. In any contest between them he was sure that she would come out on top.

He stood on the sloping lawn at the front of the house, looking down on the distant town. Suppose he were simply to leave? Pack his bags and depart for pastures new? But that drastic step would bring its own problems, not least of which would be that he would have to relinquish the job at which he had worked so long and diligently.

Surely he did not have to cease being a mortician in order to escape from his loveless marriage? There had to be a better way than that, a way in which he could free himself from Elaine while continuing to practise his craft of human dissection.

CHAPTER EIGHT

It was two days later, and little had changed, when Elaine said to him, 'By the way, I'm going to sell that bracelet thing.'

He knew immediately what she was referring to but said perversely, 'What bracelet thing?'

'The one your Aunty gave us. Don't pretend you don't know!'

He stopped pretending and gave a sigh of dismay. The bracelet was Victorian and made from pinchbeck, a copper and zinc mixture. His Aunt Agnes had given it to him on the occasion of his wedding and he had given it to Elaine who had always claimed to find it heavy and unattractive and had talked before about selling it. He dissuaded her, pointing out that it was almost a family heirloom, or anyway had been regarded as such by the maiden aunt from whom it had come.

But he did not expect a similar appeal to work this time. 'Why sell it? It'll appreciate in value if you keep it,' he said, hoping that financial considerations might sway her where sentiment would certainly fail. 'And we don't need the money.'

'I want to sell it,' she said stubbornly.

He shrugged and went on with his breakfast. There was no point in pursuing the argument. She wanted to sell it because she knew that he would want her not to do so; it was as simple as that.

'Who will you sell it to?' he asked calmly.

'Probably Armstrong's,' she said, naming a jeweller's in the town who handled second-hand items.

Coasting down the hill into town, George toyed gloomily with the idea of going to Armstrong's, or wherever she eventually sold the bracelet, and buying it back himself. Then, at least, it could be

46

produced should Aunt Agnes ever wish to see it. If it were Armstrong's, where the owner knew both Elaine and himself, what on earth would he think was going on? He would surely think it odd, anyway, that Elaine, the wife of a man known to have inherited a small fortune, should be selling her jewellery. Though that was hardly a major consideration; let him think what he liked, George would buy the bracelet back from him if he could.

Then suddenly, unbidden and for the second time, the thought of murder came into his mind. It came in the shape of a plan, a fully-fledged, detailed plan which seemed at first sight to be absolutely foolproof.

'Good God,' he said aloud in the car, swerving slightly, such was his surprise at the completeness of the thing. It took him another moment to realize that it was a plan born out of their conflict over the bracelet and her annoying decision to sell it; and, most significantly, the way in which the sale might be interpreted by others.

He stopped at the newsagents for his copy of the *Sun* and his twenty Benson & Hedges, then carried on to the mortuary, turning the plan over in his mind. There was no denying its cleverness. He did not know whether to be pleased or dismayed by this unexpected discovery of his own cunning.

That night was to be one of Elaine's parties. It was to be for the Harlequins Theatre Group, a gang of amateur thespians to which Elaine had somehow attached herself. They had been to the house before, taking it over with little cries of delight at the old billiards room, and the system of bells, that no longer worked, for summoning the servants. George knew what to expect; knew that he would have to be there but that no-one, including Elaine, would take much notice of him.

Arriving home after a day's work, during which his mind had constantly strayed back to his plan for murder, he found the preparations for the party well under way. The big pine table in the kitchen supported an impressive display of food and wine, which he knew he was forbidden to touch. Elaine, wearing a mock butcher's apron of red stripes, was cutting up french bread.

'I sold it,' were her opening words.

47

'Where?'

'Armstrong's.'

'How much did you get?'

'£180.'

This seemed to please her, although he had always believed it to be worth more. Not that it mattered. He was no longer very interested in buying it back; part of the plan with which it had provided him was that it should stay where it was.

Elaine's guests started to arrive at eight-thirty. George, upstairs in what had now been designated his bedroom, heard the first car slide to a halt on the gravel; then the echoing door-knocker and the extravagant greetings as Elaine met them in the hall.

He did not go down for some minutes. Although he had already obediently changed, he was enjoying the opportunity for solitary thought while he had the chance. He went over the plan again for the umpteenth time, now convinced of its flawlessness.

As much as anything, it had restored his self-respect. Lots of people had been attracted by the idea of the perfect murder; it was one which fiction constantly attempted but seldom achieved; and now he, George Webster, had come up with a cast-iron plan for the real thing. Whether he would have the will to carry it out was another question. A tiny voice at the back of his skull insisted that he would – that sooner or later he would find it irresistible – but he preferred for the time being to ignore it.

He finally went downstairs and said hello to a few people, some of whom clearly wondered who he was and what he was doing there.

'How're the bodies then?'

His questioner was Lawrence Cutt, a tall, bespectacled figure whose best performances were always off-stage and usually at parties.

George gave a little, noncommittal laugh.

'I was just saying to Elaine,' went on Lawrence, 'when you've got this house finished, I mean really, you know, finished, we ought to come up and give performances in the grounds. In summer of course. I don't know what, something suitable. . . .'

George did not know either.

'Perhaps something with a ghost in it. I mean if we did it at night. . . .'

'Oh, we have a ghost,' said George simply.

Lawrence registered amazement and delight on a large scale. 'You have one? A real one?'

George nodded.

'Oh well, do tell!'

But there was someone knocking at the front door. With a promise to return, George left Lawrence and made his way through the growing throng to answer it.

The cry of 'I'll get it!' came too late from Elaine as she hurried from the dining-room. George had already swung the door open and found Gordon standing there in the porch before him.

'Ah,' said Gordon, who had the good grace to be taken aback. His prepared smile subsided; he clearly recognized George, just as George recognized him, from their cross-canal encounter at The Leather Bottle.

'I said I'd get it!' hissed Elaine, arriving. Then to Gordon, 'Come in. It's all right.'

'Ah. Right. Thank you,' said Gordon, regaining something of his composure. He went past George, Elaine greeted him with a kiss that might have been excused by the theatricality of the occasion, and they went together to join the rest of the party.

As George closed the door the voice in his skull which had been insisting on the irresistibility of his murder plan crowed triumphantly.

'Now you've got to do it!' it said. 'Now you've bloody well got to!'

'Yes,' admitted George. Gordon's reaction on coming face to face with George had been as clear an admission of adultery as had ever been offered in a court of law.

'Pardon?' said Lawrence, who had come to find him. Then, before George could explain why he was talking to himself: 'What about the ghost then?'

And George, dragging his mind away from its obsession with the perfect murder of his imperfect wife, told Lawrence the story that he had heard from more than one local after he had bought the

49

house. There was supposed to be a ghost. A grey lady (weren't they always?) who appeared from time to time in the upper storey, carrying a candle and reading from the Bible.

'Have you seen her?' asked Lawrence.

'No,' admitted George.

'So who has?'

'I don't know. Nobody for quite a long time, I think.'

'So what's the story behind it?' urged Lawrence. 'Who is she?'

'I don't know that either,' said George in all honesty. None of the stories he had heard had gone into detail and, anyway, a man of George's profession could not be expected to have much interest in the supernatural.

The party was one of Elaine's more successful ones. Perhaps it was that the drama group were less staid than many of her guests on other occasions; perhaps they were more able to respond to the spirit of the house. Several of them rambled out into the gardens and could be heard shrieking at one another. Another group were shown by Elaine the secret passageway that ran from behind the dining-room fireplace to outside the house and did a conga through it. Lawrence Cutt could be heard exploring the echoes of the top-floor corridor until he hit his head on a low beam.

It was almost all over and they were starting to leave when George, who had said little to anybody for most of the time, sought out Madeleine Cummings, one of the few members of the drama group whom he had known since she was a Sister at the Infirmary.

'Madeleine,' he said.

'Hello, George.'

'You off then?' For she seemed about to leave with a couple whom George did not know.

'Yes,' she said. 'Got to get my beauty sleep, haven't I!'

'Wish I could,' said George, with what he hoped was a strained smile. 'Can't seem to get off to sleep at all nowadays.'

Madeleine gave him a sympathetic smile. She was a sweet, good-natured soul, which was what George was counting on. 'Come and see me on the Ward,' she said confidentially. 'I'll give you something that'll help.'

'Well,' said George, as if struck by the thought. 'I might do, at that.'

And they said good night as she was drawn away from him by the couple who were giving her a lift and who wanted to get away. That suited George. A hint of insomnia was all that he had wished to convey. It was a first, small step in his plan, one that committed him to nothing but which, if he were to follow things through, would form a tiny piece of the final mosaic.

The following day was a Thursday. The remains of the party, which had dragged on until the early hours, were spread throughout the house – empty bottles and cans, unwashed plates, crowded ashtrays – and everywhere a faint, clinging taste of cigarette smoke and alcohol. Elaine stayed in bed, preferring not to face it.

'Ring Mrs Bolton and ask her to come in,' she instructed George after calling him into the bedroom. Mrs Bolton was their sometimes cleaner, often called upon to deal with the aftermath of Elaine's parties.

After a breakfast of stale roll and cheese left over from the night before, George did as he was told, then went back upstairs to report to Elaine that the invaluable Mrs Bolton was on her way.

'Oh, thank God,' yawned Elaine. 'You can go now.'

In fact Mrs Bolton was not the only one with a busy day in front of her. There were two corpses already waiting for George when he arrived at the mortuary and more arrived at regular periods throughout the morning. In all, there were seven post mortems conducted that day, with the rare sight at one point of all three tables in the dissecting-room being occupied at once.

Mr Charlesworth, doing the first post mortem, confirmed the Casualty doctor's diagnosis of a perforated peptic ulcer. The man had arrived in Casualty at three o'clock that morning with agonizing abdominal pain and had died within half an hour. The second was a heart-attack – 'Myocardial infarction,' as Mr Charlesworth intoned into his cassette-recorder. And the third was the saddest of all, the only one of the day to draw expressions of sympathy from everyone working there. It was a cot death, an eighteen-month-old baby found by his anguished parents that morning. George removed the tiny organs with a care that was almost tenderness. 'Influenzeal pneumonia,' pronounced Mr Charlesworth and George put the little body into its shroud, needing no assistance from Kevin to lift it back onto its trolley.

'No more till this afternoon,' George announced after that and sent Kevin and Maurice out to the canteen for their lunch. He ate his own, as usual, in the office, content to be alone until Maurice returned after half an hour complaining about the abysmal hospital catering. George agreed, asking him to hold the fort for a while and set off for Ward Seven.

Passing through the corridors, he received a succession of small nods and salutations. They all knew him in the closed world of the hospital, and he knew them. All, as student nurses or junior doctors, had come across to the mortuary at one time or another to observe him in the practice of his craft.

Ward Seven was Female Surgical, and Madeleine Cummings was the Sister.

'Well, fancy seeing you here!' she said on seeing him.

'Couldn't sleep,' said George.

'What, now?' she laughed.

'Last night.'

'Ah,' she said, remembering their conversation. 'I'll give you a couple of Mogadon, shall I?'

'I suppose they should help, shouldn't they?' said George, looking doubtful. In fact, he wanted something stronger, as strong as he could get away with, but without having to ask for it in so many words.

'Have you had them before?' asked Madeleine.

'Yes,' he lied, 'and they don't do that much for me.'

'Well then,' she thought for a moment. 'What about Temezepan?'

'Yes, they're a bit stronger, aren't they,' he agreed. They were, indeed, a good deal stronger.

'Hang on a minute then,' said Madeleine, and went to where the medicine trolley was kept chained to a wall. Regulations decreed that dangerous drugs be kept in a locked cupboard which is itself inside another locked cupboard. The keys to both of these were safety-pinned to Madeleine's belt.

She brought him two tablets of Temezepan. He resisted the impulse to ask for more: all medical staff were alert to the dangers of dishing out potentially lethal doses of anything and he did not want this to be a transaction that she would particularly remember.

Nor did she. Ward sisters were not supposed to hand out schedule four drugs to staff who complained about not sleeping too well.

'Don't forget,' she said, half-joking, 'this isn't happening.' A proposition with which George was all too ready to agree.

He went back to an afternoon that was as busy as the morning. Mr Carter, the area's other pathologist, had taken over from Mr Charlesworth.

'It's like bloody Clapham Junction in here,' he complained.

There was another heart attack; then an old woman who had choked to death – 'Impaction of food at the glottis' was how it went down in Mr Carter's report; a Road Traffic Accident; and a woman brought straight from the operating theatre where she had died under anaesthetic.

George went home exhausted. There had certainly been little time to consider his monstrous plan further. Mrs Bolton, he noticed, had done her stuff: the house had a clean smell of polish about it, and the rubbish was tied up in a black polythene bag next to the dustbins.

'What kind of a day did you have?' he asked Elaine as she served him with a kipper and some bread and butter.

'All right,' she said, 'and I don't want to hear about yours.'

He sighed and tried another tack. 'Are you going out tonight?'

'Yes.' It was a statement of fact without even the defiance with which she would once have loaded it: they both knew now that she would do what she liked when she liked.

It was as much to have something to say as anything else that he found himself setting in motion the next stage of his plan.

'I need some money. Cash,' he said, neatly extracting a small bone from between his teeth.

She gave a little laugh. 'Don't tell me I'm supposed to get a job now!'

'No. I mean from our accounts. In fact perhaps it's best if we take some from each account instead of all from the one. I need about £5,000.'

She stared at him, giving him her full attention for perhaps the first time that week. 'Why?'

'It's a surprise,' he said. 'Something I can't tell you about yet.'

'Don't go wasting your money on anything stupid for me,' she said scornfully. 'I mean not if you're hoping it'll make me forget your slut.'

George did not retaliate at all. He replied calmly, 'No, it's nothing to do with that. It's to do with the house.'

Despite herself, she was intrigued. 'What?' she said. 'What is it?' But he shook, his head, refusing to tell her more. The more mystery, the better.

'Oh well, don't tell me then,' she said, slightly piqued, as much at his having tricked her into a show of interest as by what he would not tell her.

'But the trouble is', he went on, 'I can't get out tomorrow. I'm working all day.'

'You mean you want me to get it for you.'

'Well, if you wouldn't mind,' he said, polite and grateful. 'Only I have to have the money – cash – for this weekend.'

She said nothing. She finished the cup of coffee with which she had been toying, swilled out the cup, then made her way to the door. He kept his eyes on the evening paper by his elbow, able to follow her every move by the sound of her heels on the stone floor. They stopped in the doorway.

'Well, if you're determined to play your little game, you're going to have to tell me how much you want from where, aren't you?'

'Er, yes,' he agreed. Then added, since he had not yet decided himself and needed time to sort things out, 'I'll tell you tomorrow, shall I?'

'Suit yourself.' And the heels moved away, echoing through the hallway, then, muffled by carpet, mounting the staircase to her bedroom.

Later that night, when she had gone out, he was able to wonder just how serious he was. The concept of the perfect murder was certainly attractive; the more he thought about it, the more convinced he was that he had the means to achieve it; but, still, it needed more than that. It needed hatred, that bitter, deep hatred that will accept only the total destruction of its object. Did he hate Elaine to that degree? Or was it a hatred that was already losing its edge, dulled by their daily contact and by his abiding memory of how she had once seemed to him when she had consented to become his wife and they had stood together in the graveyard after the ceremony and he had thought himself the happiest man in the world?

'Can't go on like this though,' he said aloud.

And, indeed, they could not. Callously indifferent to each other's feelings, sleeping apart, avoiding all contact other than the minimum necessary for the house to run at all. The awfulness of the past week had become tolerable only since he had been able to see an end to it. If he were to give up now, say no and let her live, then was he not signing his own death-warrant?

He hid the two sleeping tablets in the carrying-case of his electric razor and took out his building society books in order to work out what his instructions to Elaine would be the following morning.

Once again, he had to go into her bedroom to see her before he left for work. It was becoming a regular routine, his going out before she had even deigned to climb out of bed. Perhaps she felt herself freer around the house in his absence.

'Take £1,500 out of our current account at the bank,' he told her. 'Even though there isn't much in, they won't mind a small overdraft for the time being. Then £2,000 out of this building society'–the Nationwide–'and £2,000 out of that'–the Abbey National. And he placed the passbooks on her bedside-table.

She propped herself up on one elbow and looked at him. 'You said £5,000,' she said. 'That's £5,500.'

He was not sure himself why he had increased the amount. 'Well, we might as well have plenty,' he said vaguely.

'But what the hell is it for? It is my money as well you know!'

'I'll tell you on . . . on Sunday,' he promised.

But she had had time to think about it and had evidently come up with a possible answer of her own. 'It's not for that little slut of yours, is it?' she challenged. 'You're not sending me collecting money so that you can set her up in something or other?'

'No,' he said. 'I told you that I'd never see her again and I never will.'

She lay back on her pillows and glanced through one of the passbooks that he had given her.

'It'll depend on whether I've time,' she said.

But he left her, confident that she would do as he had asked. She was, he could see, consumed with curiosity as to his purpose and would not be able to resist humouring him in order to discover it. It was a curiosity that would kill her as surely as any cat.

His day at work was again a busy one as the district seemed to be undergoing a small epidemic of death. A road traffic accident on the nearby motorway brought them its two victims; a woman died in the maternity hospital giving birth to a healthy infant; there was the inevitable heart attack and a couple of less clear-cut geriatric cases; and a man re-tiling his roof fell off it.

As well as the consequent post mortems, George now found himself conducting a delicate shuttle operation, giving each body its turn in the Chapel where it could be visited and mourned over. Some of the undertakers had their own Chapels of Rest and it was to these that some of the bodies went. Others would eventually go home, into their own front parlours, where the family traditions so dictated. But even these had to wait, residing in the cool drawers of the mortuary until their coffins were built to receive them. And often relatives wanted an early view so that these bodies, too, had to have their allocated time in the mortuary chapel. There was no time, certainly, to change the flowers. They remained the same while the bodies came and went.

There was also a small scandal erupting over the woman who had died the previous day under anaesthetic. Relatives were threatening legal action and there was the possibility of an enquiry. Not for the first time, George was reminded of the importance of his work. The Hospital Board would want to see the results of the post mortem; so, often, did the courts, solicitors and insurance companies.

At five o'clock George drove back home, up the winding road

56

that led nowhere but to the White House. Elaine was waiting for him in the dining-room.

'There,' she said, and emptied her handbag onto the table. Elastic-banded rolls of notes formed a small pyramid, then ran down the sides of it and settled, swaying gently, about the table.

'£5,500. £1,500 from the bank. £2,000 from each building society. And a real idiot I felt as well, stuffing that lot in my bag and walking around with it. I should have had a Securicor man at least!'

The money seemed to have excited her and made her talkative. For want of something more suitable, he took a coffee-pot from the sideboard and began dropping in the wads of notes. They were, he saw, £20 notes held together in what must have been £200 bunches.

'You're putting them in there!' she cried, seeing what he was doing.

'They won't be here for long. And I have to put them somewhere.'

'So are you going to tell me what you want it for now?'

'I'll tell you on Sunday.'

This amused her still more. He saw in her reaction now something of what it must have been that had originally attracted her to him, the thought of the £67,000 that he had had from Mrs Lumbley, the chance to handle it and share in major financial decisions. The glamour of all that cash had rubbed off onto him, before it had rubbed off altogether. This little adventure, with the physical presence of all that loot going into the coffee-pot, had rekindled a little of her charm and given him a glimpse of what he had once seen in her.

They even managed to dine together, though it was a modest enough meal and one during which the talk got shorter and the silences longer. He wondered whether her willingness to unwittingly connive at her own murder might not finally save her; whether this tiny show of warmth towards him, the simple recognition that they shared bank and building society accounts if not much else, might prove sufficient to deflect him from his dreadful purpose. Could he hate her enough when she was like this?

All of this came and went in his mind as he sat having a cigarette after dinner. He was now alone in the dining-room, Elaine having gone upstairs to prepare herself for the evening.

She appeared in the doorway, changed into a gaudy dress that he had not seen before and looking harder and blank-faced under a new layer of make-up.

'I'm going,' she announced.

'Where to?' he asked without thinking. It was an automatic response to her statement but one that brought a sharp retort.

'Why? What's it got to do with you?'

And, as he sought a reply that would extricate himself, she added, 'I'm going to see Gordon, if you must know.'

He gave a groan of dismay.

'Well, you would ask, wouldn't you!' she said, turned and went.

He sat without movement as he heard the door, then the car starting and going away down the hill. It was as if he were petrified by that image that her words had brought back to him: of the urbane Gordon escorting his wife from the canal boat.

It was an exchange that had repaired his resolution and sealed her fate. Whatever she might once have been, she was now so contemptuous of him as to be openly adulterous. Whatever their marriage might once have been, it was now a miserable, irredeemable sham.

The tablets had been unobtrusively obtained, the money conspicuously collected. Tomorrow was the weekend. It would, he resolved, also be the end of Elaine.

CHAPTER NINE

George was asleep before Elaine returned that night and therefore he did not see her. Nor did he see her the following morning at breakfast.

Needing to keep himself occupied, he went outside to work in the garden. It was a bright, clear day, one of the first real spring days that the year had seen. It was a day for getting jobs done, for tidying away the decay left from winter.

At ten o'clock, feeling invigorated by the exercise and the fresh air, he went back inside for a cup of coffee, and found Elaine in the kitchen. She was in her dressing-gown, evidently not long out of bed. She eyed George's caked gardening boots and his dishevelled appearance without comment.

'Good morning,' he said.

'And what's that supposed to mean?' came the icy reply.

George sighed. 'Nothing.' So poisoned was their relationship that even the most innocent expression was bound to antagonise.

'Well, and when are we going to get another gardener?' she said.

They had had one the previous year, a man who had come for two days a week and who had been working steadily to bring order out of chaos until he had resigned in protest at Elaine's criticism and peremptory commands. Since then George had done the gardening himself so that things had progressed far too slowly for Elaine's impatient designs. It seemed to him that she carried in her head a vision of a miniature Versailles and would never rest until she had the reality.

He did not reply to her question about the gardener but poured himself a cup of coffee from the percolator. It was not, anyway, a matter that would concern her for long.

'I said when are we going to get another gardener?'

'I'll, er . . . I'll put an advert in the newspaper.'

'Good. I'm tired of living in the middle of a jungle.'

George lit a cigarette. There were many things he was tired of; living in a jungle was not amongst them.

Elaine stood up. 'I'm going shopping so I'll be having lunch in town.'

George nodded, but she waited a moment, still looking at him. He looked back in surprise, wondering what could be the matter.

'So, when are you going to spend all your money then?' she said.

'Oh.' Of course. The £5,500 that she had collected for him. 'You'll see tomorrow,' he said.

She gave a little shrug and left him. Later, when he was again out in the garden, hacking away at some undergrowth with a scythe, she came out of the house, dressed smartly for a tour of the shops and stores of Arncaster. She went to her car, a green Mini that she never bothered to put in the garage and that stood outside in all weathers. George stood watching her, waiting for the chance to wave, but she steadfastly refused to look in his direction, got in the car and drove off.

So he was left alone for most of the Saturday, working hard to keep his mind off what was to come. By lunchtime he had cleared the front of the house of the dead weeds and the thin skeletal leaves that remained from the previous year and had started on the orchard, a small area of fruit trees that had degenerated into a hopeless tangle. He brought out his portable radio after lunch. It reminded him that it was the last Saturday of the football season; they were already playing the odd game of cricket. He listened to a repeat of 'Any Questions' without taking in a word of it and then some music. His mind flitted between the job in hand, the bland outpourings of the radio and the horrors to come.

It was five o'clock when Elaine's car came back up the hill and stopped in front of the house. He could stop work at last. Straightening up, it worried him to find out how frightened he was; he would need all his energies now, yet he had spent the day foolishly dissipating them on gardening.

Elaine got out of her car, then leaned back in to lift out the bags that were now full with shopping.

He hurried forward, sweaty and dirty from his exertions but wanting to catch her before she could get inside.

'Let me help you,' he called.

'It's all right,' she said. 'I can manage.' And she kicked the car door shut.

'I was just going to stop work anyway,' he said. 'Would you like a cup of tea?'

'All right,' she said, with an indifferent shrug that suggested she was only agreeing in order to humour him.

He began to see what she was thinking. That he, George, was striving to get back into favour. That the £5,500 was earmarked for some tremendous gift to her, but that none of it would work. She, Elaine, was impervious to such tactics.

He opened the door, she went past him and he followed her in. His heart was thumping, not from his day spent gardening but from the knowledge that he was now about to embark on the final and most difficult stage of his plan. Everything up to now had been retractable, had committed him to nothing. He was now about to commit murder and from that there would be no going back. Even failure would change his life forever.

'Go and make yourself comfortable,' he said, not wanting her in the kitchen. 'I'll bring it in to you.'

She gave him a quick glance, then a little smile that said that she understood what he was doing but it would not work.

'You seem very concerned about my comfort all of a sudden,' she said.

'Of course I am,' said George meekly. 'Why shouldn't I be?'

She did not answer but went out and into the lounge where he heard her putting a match to the fire that he had laid that morning. It must be cooler than he was aware. Either his day's gardening or his state of excitement and fear was keeping him warm.

He put the kettle on to boil and, leaving his gardening boots in the scullery, went quietly upstairs to the bedroom. He took out the two tablets of Temezepan from the carrying-case of his electric razor and put them in his shirt pocket.

61

He then went to the bathroom, locked himself in and opened the medicine cabinet. The bottle of Phenergan with its half-inch or so of liquid inside it was still there. He had been prescribed the full bottle some three years earlier when his state of nervous excitement at his approaching marriage had brought on an attack of urticaria. What remained now would complement the Temezepan nicely.

Going back downstairs, he peeped in through the half-open lounge door. No need to worry. Elaine was sitting before the fire, shoes off, glancing through her new copy of *Homes and Gardens*.

Once in the kitchen, he took two teaspoons and ground the Temezepan tablets to a fine powder, then poured out two cups of tea. He added sugar, the powdered Temezepan and the half-inch of Phenergan to one of them. It was a mixture that would have knocked out a horse.

So that there should be no absurd mix-up over which cup was which, he took only Elaine's with him into the lounge.

'There we are,' he said, and placed it on a small onyx table by her elbow.

'Thank you,' she said, without making any move to drink it or even looking up from her magazine.

He realized that he could not stand there watching her. He had put an extra half-spoonful of sugar in the tea but the presence of the tablets plus the Phenergan might still be faintly detectible in its taste. Anything strange about his behaviour and Elaine might well put two and two together and then everything would be lost.

So he left her there, with the cup as yet untouched, and went outside again. He had not the heart for any more gardening, though, and so simply passed a little time cleaning the scythe and the spade and the fork and the shears that he had used, putting them all in his wheelbarrow and trundling them back to that part of the dilapidated outbuildings that served as his garden shed. This took about ten minutes.

Still with time to kill, he went into the scullery through the side door and washed his hands and face, then stood and listened but could hear nothing.

Elaine was, anyway, susceptible to medications and could surely not remain conscious for very long after having swallowed the

Temezepan-Phenergan cocktail. George's only fear was that she might have forgotten altogether about the tea until it was too cold to drink. He had often complained mildly, though to no avail, about the oceans of tea and coffee that she wasted.

He looked at his watch, resolved to wait another fifteen minutes to be on the safe side, and went outside again. The afternoon was already giving way to a bright, clear evening. He sat on a large coping-stone from the collapsed gateway and smoked a cigarette.

The second hand on his watch crept round until the full fifteen minutes were finally up. George stood up and, trying to move as normally as possible in case something had gone wrong and Elaine should be there to greet him in the house, he went back inside.

His heart leapt as he came to the lounge door and saw her head lolling on one side and her body slumped in the manner of one asleep.

'Elaine?' he said, not wanting to make a mistake.

There was no response. Her mouth was open and she breathed slowly and heavily. A phrase of his grandmother's came into his mind, something she used to say to describe a deep sleep: 'the sleep of the dead'.

'Elaine?' he said more loudly and shook her by the shoulder. But she only seemed to settle deeper, her head rolling slightly and her mouth closing. She began to snore.

Satisfied that the concoction has done its job, George bent to pick her up, then stopped and straightened. He must first open all the doors so as to give himself an unimpeded journey when once he had her in his arms. He hurried out, opening the doors between lounge and garage, including the final one of the car. All, he felt, something that he should have done already: he had wasted the day gardening instead of preparing meticulously for his wife's murder.

He then went back and set himself to lift her. It was not easy. Dead weights he was used to; this living weight of his wife nearly pulled him over so that he had to let her go and she flopped back into the chair. He staggered, put out a hand to steady himself and knocked over the now empty cup. There had to be a better way. He finally found it by going down on one knee, letting her fall over his shoulder, then, holding her legs, carrying her like a sack of potatoes.

Gasping for breath, he got out of the lounge and then out of the house, and plunged on towards the garage.

If anyone had appeared or if, indeed, Elaine had staged a miraculous revival and asked him what the hell he thought he was doing, then his alibi was ready: she had fallen into apparent unconsciousness and, alarmed for her, he was rushing her to the hospital.

But no-one did appear, and Elaine was still snoring as he thankfully dropped her into the front passenger seat of his car.

The rest of it he had gone through enough times in his imagination for it to seem like the following of an already well-established routine. He took the length of rubber hosepipe that he had already cut from the endless yards that he had bought for the garden but never used. It was a piece that fitted snugly into the car's exhaust – he knew because he had tested it – then reached round so that the other end could be put through the front near-side window and the window wound up to hold it in place.

'Christ . . . !'

George cursed himself as he felt in his pockets. The car keys! Without them, of course, the car would not start, the carbon monoxide would not be produced and Elaine's snores would not be ended forever. He ran back to the house and, to his immense relief, found them in the pocket of his jacket which was hanging in the hall cupboard.

He jumped into the car, keeping his eyes averted from the hunched, sleeping figure beside him. The quicker this was done, the better, with no possibility of distracting thoughts of pity or regret that might still sabotage everything.

The engine started first time. He left the choke on full so that there would be no possibility of its cutting out. The first warm, dizzying gust of exhaust fumes were coming into the car from the pipe. George got out quickly and slammed the car door shut behind him.

He caught a last glimpse of Elaine, her mouth now open again, taking down great gusts from the piping, then he was outside in the fresh air with the garage door closed behind him. He leaned against it, feeling almost faint and in need of support. The effort had seemed tremendous and yet a greater one was still to come.

He could hear the car engine as a distant, steady roar inside the garage. Elaine would be dead within five minutes. Car exhaust fumes were over five per cent carbon monoxide; the remarkable stability of the gas meant that it accumulated rapidly in the blood stream; even in the fresh air it could prove fatal; inside the car with its minimal ventilation it would be quickly lethal.

It took him a moment to remember what was supposed to be his next step. Then he hurried indoors to the telephone, rang the hospital number and asked for Casualty. When a voice answered, he recognized it as Barbara Jennings, a staff nurse, as Irish as they come.

'Hello. Casualty?'

'Barbara. It's George Webster here.'

There was a pause. They probably, he thought, usually referred to him as 'the mortician' and found difficulty in identifying him by his name.

'Oh, hello,' she said finally. 'And what can we do for you?'

'You haven't found a book of mine, have you? Like a large desk diary with my name on the front?'

It did not seem to matter what he asked for and he waited for her to say no.

'No, er. . . .' He could imagine her peering about the office. 'No, I don't think so.'

'Oh well, never mind,' he said. 'It'll turn up. Only I came up to Casualty the other day and so I thought I might have left it there.'

'No. Sorry.'

Then, quickly, before she could ring off, he had to get in the question that mattered.

'Are you busy tonight or what?'

'No. Not yet anyway,' she said.

'Nothing for us yet?'

'Oh, goodness me, no!' she said, and laughed.

'OK,' he said. 'Bye now.' And rang off. He had heard all that he wanted to hear and now had to move without delay.

For he had chosen the time of Elaine's death carefully. Saturday was never a good day to be on call. There was too much traffic in the afternoon with the consequent high risk of accidents; and people playing sports – rugby or hang-gliding – that could have the same result. Then came Saturday night, with its drinking and fighting producing its occasional customer for the mortuary.

But between the afternoon and night there was a lull; a time when the mortician on call could count himself unlucky indeed if he were summoned by a ringing telephone. It was a time when people were at home having their teas, checking their pools coupons, smartening themselves up for the night ahead. And it was for that time that he had planned Elaine's death – when there was least chance of the mortuary being needed and of his being disturbed. Hence the cautionary telephone call to nurse Barbara Jennings: it was to ensure that nothing out of the ordinary had occurred that would result in his finding a queue of corpses at the mortuary door.

He hurried back to the garage. It was now over five minutes since he had left Elaine. The engine was roaring inside, being fed by the now unnecessary choke. George gave an instinctive glance round to check that he was unobserved, took a deep breath and opened the door.

The fumes were overpowering, even outside the car, and took him by surprise. He retreated, flung back both garage doors to let in fresh air, then, filling his lungs, dashed in again. This time he got the car door open, reached inside and switched off the engine.

Again he had to retreat into the fresh air. The fumes inside the car were so dense as to be almost tangible. Certainly Elaine was dead. She might well have died of asphyxiation before the carbon monoxide poisoning had had its effect.

As soon as he felt it safe to do so, he ran back inside and got all the doors to the car wide open. He pulled the hosepipe free and threw it into a corner. He had not yet had a proper look at Elaine; he had simply been aware of her slumped motionless in her seat. Now, seeing her properly, his practised eye told him that she was undoubtedly dead, a classic case of gas poisoning. Her face was puffy and red, her veins congested from the struggle to breathe. She had collapsed sideways across the gear column with her eyes wide open so that she seemed to be staring intently at the quartz clock on the console of the car.

The knowledge that she was dead did not affect him yet. There was still too much to be done. Her death completed only the first half of his night's work. The second would be both more arduous and risky.

Judging that the carbon monoxide would have cleared sufficiently, George got into the driving seat, re-started the car and, first easing Elaine off the gear column and back into an upright position, drove forward until the car was out of the garage and in the fresh air.

He shut off the engine; then froze in horrified disbelief as the sound of another engine reached him. It was another car pulling up at the front of the house. A sickly feeling of despair overcame him.

'Oh God,' he muttered. 'Oh please God, no.'

He was caught – caught as clearly as anyone ever had been – in the act. His wife's corpse was sitting in the front seat of his car, which he had just driven out of a garage still reeking of exhaust gases.

The other car had stopped and he heard its doors being swung open.

Coming to life, he jumped from his own car and hurried forward. Better to catch whoever had arrived at the front of the house than have them come investigating.

It was Pat Davenport, a friend of Elaine's, of about Elaine's age and, for that matter, with the same inclination towards money and the good life. She had just got out of her Lotus Elan and gave a small start of surprise as George came round the side of the house towards her.

'Oh, hello. Elaine in?'

'No,' he said, shaking his head. 'No, she's . . . she's out.'

'Ah,' said Pat.

She seemed dissatisfied, as if she did not fully believe him. Then he noticed, as she had done already, the green Mini parked by the front door.

'I think she took a taxi,' he said, a touch wildly. 'I haven't a clue where she was going. You know Elaine . . . !' And a hopeful laugh.

This, mercifully, seemed to satisfy Pat.

'Oh well, never mind,' she said, but then, before he could stop her, she had come past him, her attention caught by something in the garden behind him.

'Your poinsettia's doing well,' she exclaimed, and bent to examine its long, scarlet leaves.

'Yes,' he agreed hastily and moved in a hopeless attempt to block her view.

For, as she straightened up, she could now see down the side of the house to where the Volvo, its doors open, was parked in front of the garage. The Volvo in which he had left Elaine, propped upright in the front seat.

He knew that she had seen the car, could not have avoided seeing it. His own breathing stopped as he waited for her cry. But none came.

'Oh well,' she said. 'If you could tell her that I called.'

It was only then that he dared look himself; and saw the blank windscreen where Elaine's head should have been framed in full view. She had gone.

He must have said goodbye to Pat without being aware of it, for she went back to the Lotus and, pulling it round in a tight circle that left tracks in the gravel, accelerated away through the gate and down the hill.

George turned and went fearfully back to the Volvo. Getting close, he could still see nothing. If Elaine were alive . . . ? If she had stumbled out and were now trying to escape him. . . . Then, as he looked inside, all became clear and he gasped with relief.

She had slumped sideways again across the gear column. Even as he had been talking to Pat, she must have slid gently out of view and thus saved him from discovery.

'Thank God,' he said aloud.

The nearness of his escape spurred him into a fresh burst of activity. He opened the tailgate at the back of the car. It was relatively easy, now that she was lifeless, to lift Elaine out, carry her round and lay her on the floor behind the back seat. An old rug from the garage covered her and he could close the tailgate. They were now ready to go.

He locked up the house and the garage, checked that the body was well covered and got into the driver's seat. The exhaust gases seemed to have completely dispersed so that he felt safe in closing the window and driving carefully away, down into the quiet streets of the town towards the hospital.

The mortuary stood by itself, somewhat apart from the main block of the hospital buildings and hidden from them by a tactfully placed group of beech trees. George pulled into his usual parking-place, glad to see that there was no other car there. Kevin was the mortuary attendant on call. Although there would now normally be no post mortems before Monday morning, he would be the one summoned if a body arrived for admission.

But none had arrived yet. Kevin's old Volkswagen Beetle was nowhere to be seen, and when George tried the door to the mortuary it was locked.

Clever as his plan was, it contained moments of risk that could not be avoided. Lifting Elaine's body from the car and into the mortuary was one of them. He backed up the car tight against the door, wrapped the rug around the body, then, with one great heave, almost threw it inside.

He felt better once he could close and lock the mortuary door, though he knew that it would not keep out Kevin, who had a key of his own, or hide his car, which was standing outside for anyone who cared to look.

At least he did not need to hump Elaine around anymore. It was much easier to bring a trolley, lift her onto it and, getting his breath back, wheel her through to the dissecting-room.

His familiarity with the place, and with the processes of death, allowed him to go ahead swiftly with the next part of his plan, not flinching at the gloom and cold of the room or the thin echo that every movement produced. He did not want to switch on the lights, or at least none that could be seen from the window. Perhaps the single, adjustable lamp over the table might be safe. He switched it on, then rolled Elaine from the trolley into its chilly glare.

He would need the usual tools of his trade – knives, basins and necropsy saw – and a supply of plastic bags, the ones usually used

69

for holding the possessions of accident victims. Having assembled these, he put on a gown, wellingtons and a pair of thin rubber gloves. He was now ready to take his wife apart.

Strangely, the most difficult step was removing her clothes. Stripping her seemed a more obscene violation than had the murder. However, once it had been done and the clothes had gone into the first of the black bags, she resembled the thousands of other bodies that he had looked down on over the years. Only a few details of facial bone structure identified her as his wife: in everything else she was unremarkable.

It was still quite a task. For the next half-hour he worked quickly and skilfully, hurried on by the thought that this was the most dangerous time of all, that if Kevin or one of the pathologists were to come in on some errand then he would be caught red-handed, literally so once he had made the first cuts and the blood had started to flow down the channels in the table and away to the gulleys at his feet.

In the end he had fifteen black bags, tightly fastened and of varying shapes and sizes. The most innocent contained her clothes and shoes. The largest her head. Two others, long and thin, contained an arm each, taken off by the ball-and-socket joint at the shoulder. The torso he had divided down the midline and across beneath the rib-cage into four. Each quarter had gone into its own black bag, another of which had been needed for the bowels, stomach and membranes. Then another six bags altogether for the thighs, legs and feet. Making fifteen. They formed a small pile on the floor, only the odd smear of blood betraying the contents.

For a time he was so lost in concentration as to forget the gruesome nature of his task. He had noted with a professional eye the effects of the carbon-monoxide poisoning and the consequent asphyxiation – the brightly-tinted blood and the intrapulmonary haemorrhages – about which he could have produced his own post mortem report unaided.

Now, as he tied a last foot into its bag, he had time to contemplate what he had done, and the enormity of it came home to him.

'I had to,' he said aloud, defensively. 'Had to.'

His words were picked up by the whisper of an echo: 'Had to . . . had to . . .'

He breathed deeply, trying to steady himself. His body trembled from a combination of exhaustion and revulsion. But another ten minutes and the worst would be over. He could not afford the luxury of self-examination with his wife's remains parcelled up beside him. Using his foot, he switched on the water tap and played the jet about the table, swilling away the blood and gore. Then he scrubbed it and cleaned around the gulleys and the floor beneath. He cleaned the instruments, returning each to its alloted place. He took off his wellingtons and put his blood-stained gown in the laundry skip.

He then put Elaine, piece by piece, back on the trolley on which he had wheeled her in.

The refrigerated drawers in which the bodies were kept each had its own key and its own number. George opened number seven, transferred the bags into it, closed it and then locked it again. The key then went into his pocket instead of back into the office as was customary. From that moment he felt safe from discovery. If Maurice or Kevin should notice either the missing key or the locked drawer, which was unlikely, they would accept without question George's explanation that it was faulty and temporarily out of commission.

He returned to the dissecting-room before leaving, anxious that he should have left no sign of his work there. The wet table and area around were already drying. Certainly by the time the first post mortem was held on Monday morning there would be nothing to incriminate him.

He locked up the mortuary and got back into his car. He was unable to believe what he had achieved; that he had dared so much and got away with it. Elaine was dead. She was also under lock and key and safe from discovery. There had been no witnesses.

Driving home, he felt light-headed from a mixture of exhilaration and relief. And also fear – a fear that had no immediate cause but that he would come to recognise as the distant, ever-present reminder that he would always have something to hide.

Around him the town was coming to life for the evening, people were going to bingo or to dance halls and the pubs were filling up. It surprised him that so little had been changed by his act of murder. The White House, too, seemed no different from when he had left it – except for the telephone, which was ringing as he came through the door.

He went to answer it, hesitated, told himself that he had nothing to fear, and picked up the receiver.

'Hello?' he said.

There was no answer. Just a moment's pause and then the phone at the other end was put down.

George frowned, wondering what it could mean. His head filled with wild ideas: that he had been detected; that the call was a warning, a signal that someone knew. But none of the ideas made much sense, even to his excited imagination. All he really knew was that someone had rung and had then put the phone down without speaking.

That one thing apart though, he could now relax. He poured himself a large whisky, opened the french windows and sat in front of them overlooking the garden. So weak was he after his great effort that the alcohol seemed to burn its way into him. He drank some more, feeling the need for its numbing infusion.

But he felt no regret. It pleased him to find not a trace of regret that Elaine was now dead. A deposit of fear, yes; surprise at his own daring; relief that it was over; a sense of gratitude for the luck that had been with him when he had needed it. But no regret. Rather a sense of emancipation. Escape.

The telephone rang again. He answered it and this time there was a voice, a voice that he recognized but could not immediately place.

'Hello?' it said.

'Hello,' said George.

'Could I speak to Elaine, please?'

This gave him the clue that he needed. It was Gordon. Gordon phoning from his canal boat, if such a thing were possible. It immediately made sense of the earlier call, which presumably had also been Gordon, hoping that Elaine would answer and not wanting to have to speak to George. Evidently he had now thought about it and decided that he had little alternative.

'She's not here,' said George.

'Oh. Er, you don't know where she is by any chance, do you?'

It was an impertinent question for a man to ask his lover's husband but one that George on this occasion was only too happy to answer.

'No, I don't' he said. 'She went out this afternoon and hasn't been back since.' Which tied in with what he had said to Pat and would help to establish a pattern of movements for Elaine should anyone ever set out to uncover them.

'I see.'

There was a pause. Obviously they had arranged to meet and Elaine had not shown up.

'I'll tell her you called, shall I?' asked George, now quite in charge of the situation.

'Yes,' said Gordon. 'Thank you.' And he rang off.

George gave a little laugh of triumph.

CHAPTER TEN

Over the years George had participated in the post mortems of five cases of proven murder, and several more might-have-beens. He was familiar with the Coroner and with his ways of thinking. He was also familiar with the police and with their ways of thinking.

Of two things he was quite sure. One – that for a murder investigation to even get off the ground there had to be a body or part of a body. And two – that such investigations always began by looking for motives. Who had wanted him or her dead? Who would have had most to gain from the death?

George's belief that he had committed the perfect murder was based on the facts that no body would ever be found and that, far from having benefited from Elaine's disappearance, he would be the person generally seen to have lost most by it – to have been left for a sucker by a wife who had taken the money and run.

Hence the £5,500 that he had sent Elaine collecting. If anyone should ever investigate her disappearance they would find that, immediately prior to it, she sold a pinchbeck bracelet for £180, then went round the banks and buildings societies of the town collecting some thousands of pounds more. Clearly the actions of a woman about to scarper. Then there would be other corroborative evidence. Her affair with Gordon must have been the subject of gossip, and she must, he was sure, have often confided in her friends her dissatisfaction with her marriage to George. The evidence would be overwhelming that she had left him of her own accord. Few people would be surprised. Some, no doubt, would claim to have expected it; would say that they were only surprised that she had not gone earlier.

George spent a quiet Sunday reading the newspapers, watching television and performing the few small tasks that remained to make his alibi watertight. Elaine's jewellery, which she would certainly have taken with her, he dropped into the well that had once brought water to the now derelict greenhouses at the bottom of the garden. He smashed the empty Phenergan bottle and threw the fragments away. And, finally, he let down the front off-side tyre of the Mini.

Monday morning was work as usual. George collected his cigarettes and his copy of the *Sun* and arrived at the mortuary to find everything undisturbed since his visit on the Saturday night.

Maurice arrived two minutes after him.

'And how are you, George? Have a good weekend?' he asked.

'To tell you the truth,' said George, in the manner of one relieved to be able to confide in an old friend, 'it was about the worst weekend of my life.'

'No . . . !' said Maurice, taken aback. 'What happened?'

'Elaine's gone. Left me. At least I presume she has. On Saturday afternoon. Took some of her things and . . . just went.'

It was better, he had decided, that the news should be spread as quickly as possible. Elaine would certainly be missed: better that people heard his version of things before they could jump to their own conclusions.

They had a cup of tea and a smoke in the office while Maurice sympathised. Kevin, who arrived later, was sent to cope alone with the first of the morning's customers.

'She might come back', mused Maurice sympathetically, 'once she realizes how stupid she's been.'

'No, I don't think so,' said George. 'The way things have been between us lately, I don't think I shall ever see her again.'

Maurice, faced with this unaccustomed insight into someone else's emotional life, could only shake his head in dismay.

One last step of George's plan remained to be taken – one on which everything else depended. The body, although dissected, polythene-wrapped and safely stored away, still had to be disposed of. It was a process that he knew might take some time to complete but that he was able to begin that same afternoon.

Mrs May Hammond had died three days earlier. She had been trying to reach a new packet of budgerigar food from the top shelf of her pantry when the stool on which she was standing slipped. She had fallen, broken her collar-bone, suffered a massive heart attack and died within seconds. A post mortem had been duly carried out and the Coroner had given permission for burial. Her coffin arrived after lunch and George and Kevin between them transferred her into it from the refrigerated drawer in which she had been residing. She was then placed in the mortuary Chapel where the few friends and relations that she had might visit her before she was buried the following morning.

At three-thirty, with things being quiet, George sent Maurice and Kevin off together for their tea-break.

Then, first locking the mortuary door as a precaution against being disturbed, he went to drawer number seven, the drawer in which Elaine was stored. Opening it, he hesitated for a moment, wondering which parcel to take but then, realizing that it made no difference whatsoever – each was equally damning and in the end all would have to be disposed of – he lifted out the nearest one. He then closed and re-locked the drawer.

Taking the parcel to the Chapel, he judged from the feel of it that he had got part of the torso.

Mrs Hammond had never in her life been overweight. Now, in her death at the age of sixty-eight, she weighed only six stone. There was plenty of room in her coffin for a small part of Elaine.

George wedged the parcel in down at the bottom, by Mrs Hammond's legs, rearranged the shroud, and stood back. There was nothing to show that the coffin and its contents had been added to and the extra weight would be so small as to be undetectable. Only the most absurd misfortune could now bring about discovery.

And none did. Mrs Hammond was buried the following morning in the town cemetery. There were few mourners, the service was short and the weather wet and windy. The cars had barely left the cemetery gates before the two gravediggers were hurrying forward with their shovels to bury forever the whole of Mrs Hammond and the one-fourteenth part of Elaine.

It was by this method that George would ensure that there would be no body for someone to stumble upon. He would use his unique situation as mortician to spirit his wife away piece by piece, in the company of those deceased with whom he had his professional dealings.

At home that night the telephone calls began, as he had known that they must.

'Hello,' said Pat, who was the first. 'Can I speak to Elaine?'

'No, sorry,' said George. 'She's not here.'

'Do you know when she will be?' came the plainly dissatisfied response.

'Look, I might as well tell you,' said George. 'She's gone. You know when I told you that she'd set off on Saturday afternoon? Well, I haven't seen her since. Whether I ever will I've no idea.'

There was a pause as Pat sought a suitable reaction. 'Oh dear,' was all that she could finally manage.

'So there. You might as well know the truth. Everybody will sooner or later.'

She managed a few more half-baked expressions of surprise and consolation and rang off. He could imagine her eagerness to spread the delightful scandal and hoped that she would be successful in doing so. It would save him the job.

Nevertheless, his little performance as the shocked and upset husband so abruptly deserted by his wife was one that he had to give several more times before the week was out. Even those who already knew seemed to want to find a pretext for ringing him.

'Sorry to bother you, George. Just wondered if you'd heard anything from Elaine yet?'

'No, nothing. Don't suppose I will either,' became his stock answer.

Meanwhile he worked carefully and steadily to dispose of the remaining fourteen bags.

The head, being the largest, was the only one to present real difficulties. He tried unsuccessfully to fit it into three coffins before finding one that would take it. Even then, it spoiled the line of the shroud ever so slightly, and he was relieved to see the lid of the coffin go on and the undertaker drive away with it without anyone being any the wiser.

A second section of the torso, then the left arm and then a foot all went on their way in the company of bodies that were to be cremated. The bag containing the clothes and shoes went to the town's Roman Catholic cemetery and had a requiem mass said over it. The right thigh went to Bradford for burial: the deceased in question had moved from there some years before and had asked to be returned to the family vault after his death. Another bag, containing a section of leg, went to the town cemetery so that by the end of the week there were seven bags remaining, just less than half of the original total.

It was then that George made his visit to the police. He had considered the matter carefully and decided that it was in his interest to do so. There seemed no possibility of their discovering anything incriminating; it could only help to establish his role as the distressed husband.

He went on the Saturday morning and was seen by a woman police sergeant.

'There's actually very little we can do,' she said, after he had explained about Elaine's disappearance.

He sighed. 'I know you can't make her come back.'

'Well, exactly. Unless you suspect that there might be anything, well, suspicious about your wife's departure then there isn't, strictly speaking, any reason for us to become involved.'

'I just thought,' said George, 'if I could only find out where she was, then I'd be easier in my mind.'

She gave him a sympathetic smile. 'All that I can do', she said, 'is add her name to our missing persons list. Then, if she is in contact with any police force for any reason they would at least let us know. And we could let you know that she was all right.'

'That's what I'd hoped,' said George, a picture of gratitude.

'But even so,' warned the woman police sergeant, 'unless she gave us permission we wouldn't be able to tell you where she was. I mean, give you her address or anything.'

'I understand,' said George.

'Now. I'll just take down the details.'

And George went through his story again, not forgetting to

78

mention the trips to the banks and the building societies. He had of course been unaware of these at the time, he said, but they now clearly showed that her departure was premeditated. He also hesitantly confessed to the knowledge that Elaine had had a lover, Gordon, canal boat owner and member of the Harlequins Theatre Group.

'Would he know where she might be?' asked the woman police sergeant.

'I don't know,' said George, frowning, as if struck for the first time by such a possibility.

He would certainly not object to Gordon's being under suspicion. Perhaps the police would go so far as to visit and question him. There would be a certain justice about Gordon's being discomfited.

It took a further nine days to dispose of the rest of Elaine. The remaining quarters of the torso went to the town cemetery; the bag containing the stomach, bowels and membranes was cremated. The left thigh travelled to the small cemetery surrounding the stone chapel that had been the Methodist foothold in the town since early Victorian times. This left George with only two bags still secreted in drawer seven. Oddly, they gave him the greatest difficulty of all. Circumstances just never seemed right: either there was no body in the Chapel at all or, when there was, he was never alone long enough to take advantage of it. He made a surreptitious return late one night but found Mr Charlesworth there before him collecting some samples. He resolved instead to come in early the following morning, thinking that he could transfer a bag before anyone else arrived. However, he was frustrated again, finding the undertaker already waiting to take the body away.

Finally, though, his run of bad luck ended and he was able to complete the task. A section of leg went to be cremated in the company of a young man killed when his motor-bike had failed to take a corner. And, last of all, the right foot went to the town cemetery in what proved to be the biggest send-off of the lot. The deceased whom it accompanied had once been a gypsy, a genuine traveller, before she had developed sciatica and settled in a house in

Arncaster. Now over sixty members of her far-flung family congregated in their caravans and wagons to lay her to rest. It was a colourful procession and seemed to George, who watched it from afar, to be a suitable celebration of his own triumph.

It had been during that second week that he had received a telephone call from an irate Gordon.

'What have you been telling the police?' he demanded.

'Why?' asked George.

'Because they've just been round here, suggesting that I might know something about your wife's going off or whatever it is that she's done!'

George remained calm, surprised but not displeased that the police should have gone to such lengths.

'And don't you?' he asked.

'No, I do not!'

'Well, you've got nothing to worry about then, have you.'

And he was gratified to hear the receiver being sharply replaced at the other end of the line.

When he heard no more, either from Gordon or from the police, it encouraged him to think that their investigations had led them nowhere and that they had therefore no cause to doubt his story that Elaine had upped and left him.

Drawer seven was now empty. He returned the key to the office alongside the others. It was over. Elaine was dead and buried. What was more, she had been buried and cremated in the authorized fashion, not left rotting in some trunk or hastily hidden in nearby woodland. His undertaker colleagues had often philosophised on the importance of the funeral service in signalling an acceptable end to the life of a loved one. George, whose wife had now shared in fourteen funeral services of different kinds, felt calm and contented.

There now remained for him only the task of adjusting to his new life and deciding what course it should take. He still had the White House to keep in good order, even if he did not have Elaine driving him on to ever grander schemes. Perhaps he should try and sell it? Or, at any rate, find a housekeeper to keep it clean and tidy until he made his mind up as to just what he did want to do with it.

It had taken him a little over two weeks to dispose of Elaine. It would be another week before Martyn Culley would arrive in the town to stay with Rob and Samantha. And a further two days before the police would come visiting to try and establish the identity of a woman whose body had been washed ashore on a Devon beach.

CHAPTER ELEVEN

The Friar Tuck was the kind of restaurant that, without ever being busy, was never deserted. It was as if a pool of undernourished extras took it in turns to keep the place ticking over.

There were three of them, each sitting alone at separate tables, when George came in. He went and sat by the fish-tank, in which he could see the kitchen door reflected. It was from here that Josie would come, if she were on duty; and, indeed, if she were still in the job at all.

It had been a quiet day at the mortuary. He had taken a chair out into the sunshine for an hour in the afternoon and then been mildly embarrassed by falling asleep and having to be awakened by an amused Kevin. Now, rather than going back to his lonely house and the business of preparing a meal for himself, he had decided to eat out. Besides which, he had an ulterior motive.

Josie finally, reluctantly, appeared and slouched across towards him. She was wearing the same blouse and skirt that seemed tighter then ever.

'Hello,' he said, turning to her.

She had not recognized him and was thrown for a moment. She recovered enough to give a little sneer of contempt and fairly threw the menu down on the table.

'Oh, it's you, is it!'

'I hoped you'd still be here,' said George, undeterred. He could hardly have expected much of a welcome.

'Oh yeah? Why, you're going to ask me out again, are you?'

At least, he noticed, she was keeping her voice down, which suggested that her disgust with him was mechanical, the only reaction she could summon up on finding him there. The experience of being picked up and then hastily abandoned was perhaps in line with her experience of most things in life.

'I'm sorry about what happened before,' he said meekly.

She gave a 'Huh' of contempt, as though anything that could ever happen involving him was of sublime indifference to her.

'Are you still looking for another job?'

'Not with you, no!'

Again it was all he could have expected.

'Well,' he said, studying the dog-eared menu, 'I can offer you one if you are. And it'd have accommodation going with it.'

She said nothing, which was enough to encourage him to go on. 'Do you know Old Moore's Hill, out towards Harrington?'

'Might do,' she said, which meant that she did.

'Well, you know the White House when you get right to the top of that road?'

'Are you going to order or what?' she said.

'Er, yes. I'll have a soup of the day, then plaice and chips. Oh, and a glass of pale ale please.'

She did not go immediately but stayed, writing down his order on a small pad.

'You know the house?' he repeated.

'Might do.'

'Only I live there. And I need a housekeeper.'

She looked at him. 'What, you mean cleaning?'

'Oh, a lot more than cleaning. In fact, I have a cleaner comes in sometimes already. No, I mean run the whole house. It's a much more responsible job than just being a cleaner.'

'I'm not going to be anybody's cleaner,' she said and, taking the menu, went back into the kitchens.

He wondered whether that meant that she was interested or not. He had said that he did not want a cleaner and she had said that she did not want to be a cleaner. So perhaps there was a chance after all.

A party of four came into the restaurant causing a small bustle so there was a spell when she was busy, stopping only briefly by his table to deliver first the soup and then the plaice and chips. She seemed to have forgotten the pale ale and he did not like to ask for

83

it. It was only when she came to take away his empty plate that he had the chance to speak to her again.

'Look, why don't we just have a talk about it? Then you can see whether you're interested.'

'Oh yeah? Go out for a drink and have your wife turn up again?' she sneered defensively.

'No, my wife's gone,' he said calmly. 'There's no chance of her turning up again.'

She gave him a puzzled look, took the plate and went back through the double-hinged doors into the kitchen.

When he went to the till to pay, a small, thin-faced man in his shirt-sleeves came scuttling out to attend to him so George had no option but to leave without seeing any more of Josie. This, presumably, was what she had intended.

In truth, the idea of inviting her to be his housekeeper had come to him only that afternoon in the form of an erotic dream as he had dozed in the sunshine outside the mortuary. Josie in the dream had been wearing an apron and little else and he had chased her up the stairs and along the first floor corridor. Awakening, he had wondered, why not? He needed a housekeeper. He perhaps needed some love in his life as well. She, as she had told him that fateful night outside The Leather Bottle, needed a new job and some accommodation to go with it. It might work out. What had he got to lose?

Certainly, the White House seemed bigger and emptier than ever these days. He spent the rest of the night sitting alone, watching television and sipping whisky until the announcer bade him good night and the screen went blank.

'Morning,' said Kevin, meeting him the following morning as he unlocked the mortuary door. 'You look like you had a late night.'

'Oh, do I,' said George stiffly. He had noticed that his young assistant was beginning to patronise him, treating him as a venerable figure to be jokily played along. Responding irritably, he worked Kevin hard all the morning, and himself even harder.

He also resolved to try Josie again; give her one last chance. It was her youthfulness as much as anything that he needed in his life.

'Anything exciting lined up for tonight then?' asked Kevin as they prepared to leave at the end of the afternoon.

'You'd be surprised,' said George.

Kevin laughed. They went to their respective cars and it pleased George, as he pulled away in his Volvo, to see Kevin having trouble starting the old Volkswagen.

He went home, made himself a toasted cheese sandwich and ate it while watching the news on television. Then, judging that the time was right, he went out again, drove to the restaurant and parked in the street outside – in fact, in the same spot where he had waited for her before.

She came out bang on seven-thirty and he was glad to see that she was alone. He tapped gently on his horn so that it gave a discreet honk which brought her head round to look at the car. She recognised it. Her step faltered for a moment, then she came on towards him.

He pressed a button that lowered the nearside window. She came to it and leaned down to look in at him. She was chewing chewing-gum and reminded him of all the gangsters' molls that he had seen in the American films of his youth.

'You don't give up easy, do you?' she said laconically. It was a line she must have composed on her way to the car.

'Let's go and have a drink and we'll talk about that job,' said George evenly. His best chance, he thought, lay in being careful not to be persuasive or pushy. Just hold out the offer to her for her to accept or reject as she pleased.

'Oh yeah,' she jeered. 'What, that canal place again?' But she did not move away.

'Anywhere you like,' he said, and, leaning across, opened the door for her.

His heart gave a little leap of excitement as she got in, showing a fair expanse of thigh in the process. He was, he recognized, hopelessly in love with her. At that moment he would have given her anything, betrayed anyone for the chance of having his love returned. He started the car and drove off without knowing where he was going.

'I suppose you've eaten,' he said.

'I suppose I have,' she said.

They travelled another half-mile with the car seeming to find its own way before an idea struck him.

'Would you like to see the house?'

'What? Your house?'

'Yes.'

She gave a little laugh of derision. 'Not bothering with the drink this time then, are we?'

'We can go for a drink afterwards,' he said. 'I only mean call in for five minutes so that you can see what the job would be. That's if you're interested.'

She did not reply but glanced sideways at him as if trying to assess what she might be letting herself in for. Perhaps the slightness of his build reassured her. Or perhaps it was the St Christopher medal stuck magnetically onto the dashboard of the car.

'If you like,' she said finally.

George felt another thrill of sexual excitement. She was going to agree. He knew she was. If he just played his cards right she was going to agree to the whole thing.

'Oh, this,' she said in recognition as they drove in through the gateway. 'I always wondered who lived here.'

'It still needs a lot doing to it,' he said. It had become his automatic, apologetic first line to every visitor over the past three years. It was the kind of house that would always need a lot doing to it.

She needed no further encouragement to leave the car and follow him indoors. Perhaps the size of the house alone offered some sort of guarantee that she would not be molested. At least it made sense of the idea of a housekeeper.

'And is your wife really not here any more?' she asked him as they came first into the kitchen.

'No,' he said. 'She's gone.'

'Gone where?'

'I don't know,' said George. 'But I'm sure she's not coming back.'

'How can you be sure she's not coming back if you don't know where she's gone?'

86

It was a fair question.

'Because I wouldn't have her back,' he answered a trifle wildly. 'Even if she asked to come back I wouldn't have her back.'

This seemed to satisfy her. They continued on their tour of the house.

'That's the original fireplace,' said George as they stood in the lounge. '1634. It's got the date carved on the stone just inside here. Look.'

But she was not very interested in dates and looked instead at the pile of wood and coal waiting there to be lit. 'So I'd have to clean this out every morning, would I?'

'Well,' he said, 'only if there'd been a fire the night before. There is central heating as well.'

The sitting-room and dining-room impressed her but not by their antiquity. It was here that Elaine had most nearly achieved what she had set out to: they were fully carpeted, re-decorated and comfortable, with ample, expensive furniture.

She followed George upstairs without demur. The house had captured her curiosity and for a time at least she forgot to be worldly and cynical. She peered in, wide-eyed, through the doors as George pointed out the bedroom which had been Elaine's and then the one that was his own.

'You had different rooms then?' she exclaimed in surprise.

'Yes,' he said. 'There wasn't much point in not having them.'

'You were still married though, weren't you?'

'Not in a way that meant very much.'

This insight into his unhappiness seemed to catch her imagination and she gave him a quick glance of sympathy.

'Must have been awful for you.'

'Yes,' he agreed, wondering now if it really had been as bad as all that.

His present torment was bad enough: to be leading this nubile little miss from bedroom to bedroom with his body aching for her and yet able only to talk about the past in terms of Elaine or the present in terms of household maintenance. Telling himself that satisfaction delayed would be all the sweeter, he showed her the airing-cupboard and the workings of the immersion heater.

They went upstairs again to the other, unused bedrooms. Here, even in the warm spell of weather that they were having, the air was tainted with damp which had stained the walls in large patches.

'Spooky isn't it?' she said.

'It needs decorating, that's all really,' said George, trying to make light of it. He was certainly not going to embark on the story of the ghost and risk having her flee the house there and then.

They came lastly to the end window which looked out over the gardens.

'And is all that yours?'

'Yes,' he said. 'Well, as far as that wall that you can see beyond those trees.'

'Christ,' she said in a small voice. The White House, so far outside of her experience and her expectations, seemed to have overwhelmed her.

'Let's go and have that drink then, shall we?' he said, now anxious to hurry her out before she should decide that the whole thing was too much, that she would feel out of place and intimidated by it all.

They were going out through the hall when she stopped and asked, 'Suppose I did come here, where would I be sleeping?'

He hesitated. The idea of her coming at all had been such a recent one that he had not yet got round to working out the nuts and bolts of the situation.

'Oh, anywhere you wanted, I suppose,' he said.

She had been so far disarmed by the house that she did no more than nod in reply.

They went to another pub this time, the Admiral Lord Rodney. As he bought them drinks, she retired to the ladies. When she came back it seemed that her defences had been restored. She had had time to reflect on how other people would view her moving into the White House and wanted him to know that she was no fool.

'I mean, let's get this clear,' she said, leaning forward over her Bacardi and Coke. 'You want me to come and be what you call a housekeeper. And nothing else? I mean let's be honest. That's all I'm coming for, right?'

'Right,' agreed George, excusing the lie to himself on the grounds that, yes, it was all that she was coming for initially. If things developed afterwards then that would not really be his fault, would it?

They talked about a salary and time off.

'Can you drive?' he asked her.

'Yes.'

'Oh good.'

'Why?'

'Oh, just that, with the house being a fair way out of town, it'll be useful if you can use the car.'

She hesitated, then said, 'I haven't got a licence though. I mean I've never taken a test.'

It was his turn to hesitate. 'Well, perhaps you could then. If you wanted to.'

He could see that, as time passed, the spell of the house was wearing off. She began to glance round, increasingly aware of who might be there seeing her with him. For his part he had no such qualms. His perfect murder – for he was now convinced that that was what it was – had given him a self-confidence, even a touch of arrogance, that had not been there before. Let people think what they liked. He had for too long let other people – or at any rate one other person in particular – rule his life. He would now please himself.

(It had even crossed his mind to leave some kind of letter, to be opened after his death, boasting of how he had killed Elaine and got away with it. He had not yet gone into the idea enough to decide whether it would be wise or just how it could best be managed. But it seemed a shame that his secret might go to the grave with him.)

'Tell you what,' said Josie, swigging back her fourth Bacardi and Coke, 'I'll give you a ring, shall I?'

'When?'

'Well, when I've had time to think about it. Tomorrow. Or the day after.'

It was, as he had feared, that she was going off the idea.

'Well, is there really all that much to talk about?' he urged. 'I mean I thought you liked the idea.'

'It's a big step, isn't it,' she said. 'Give me your number and I'll give you a ring.'

In the end he had to do that. He gave her both his home number and his number at the mortuary. Doing so, he remembered that he had lied to her about his job, had told her that he was in hospital administration. But the number he gave her, an extension from the main hospital switchboard, would tell her nothing in itself. Even were she ever to call him on it! Writing the numbers down for her on the back of a cigarette packet, he felt sure that he would hear nothing, that the moment had passed and he would never see her again.

The following morning was taken up by two post mortems conducted by Mr Charlesworth. Standing there watching the pathologist going through his familiar routine, it struck George how many other perfect murders there might be besides his own. It had not, after all, been difficult. And other people were in privileged positions beside himself: coroners, doctors, undertakers. . . . Perhaps there were a good many more perfect murders than was generally recognized.

There were few such chances for speculation though: the morning was a busy one. Maurice was away ill and so they were short-staffed. There was no time for George to send Kevin out for sandwiches for his lunch. Instead, he had to take twenty minutes off to rush up to the canteen himself. By this time it was one-thirty, the menu was depleted and they had to make him an omelette.

'There was a phone call for you,' said Kevin, when he got back to the mortuary.

'Who was it?' said George, suddenly reminded of Josie and her promise that she would ring.

'They didn't say. I said you'd be back in half an hour and they said they'd ring again.'

'Was it a man or a woman?'

'A man,' said Kevin, surprised at the question.

George, disappointed by the answer, went to make himself a cup of tea on the electric kettle in his office. It was probably not Josie then. Unless it was her boss ringing to complain about the poaching of his staff. Or her probation officer? He wondered, not for the first time, whether he had been wise in contacting her again.

He had made the tea and was putting in the sugar when the telephone rang.

'Hello. Mortuary,' he said.

'Mr Webster?'

'Yes.'

'Ah. Good afternoon, sir. It's Arncaster police station here.'

This did not, in itself, worry him unduly. The police and George were frequently in touch on professional matters that concerned them both. Except that this time it was different.

'It's about your wife, sir.'

George's heart gave a little leap. He said nothing because everything he could think of saying might have been wrong. He waited.

'Or rather it may be about your wife,' went on the voice from the police station. 'She is still missing, is she?'

He relaxed somewhat. If they were not sure that she was missing then there was not much else that they could be sure of.

'Could somebody come and see you do you think? Just have a word with you about it?'

'Er, yes, of course.'

'It might be best if we came to your home. What would be the best time, sir?'

Seven o'clock that evening was agreed upon. George left the mortuary for home as soon as he could decently get away, feeling a vague need to check the house and grounds before the police arrived. He wandered round the garage, found the length of rubber hose and tucked it inside a tea-chest that was full of odds and ends. Inside the house there was still plenty of evidence of Elaine's having been there – clothes in her wardrobe, her coats in the hall – but that was only as it should be.

Two policemen arrived on time in an unmarked Ford Escort. They themselves were not in uniform. He watched them from the windows as they came from their car looking round at the house and grounds, one of them saying something that made the other one laugh. He recognized neither of them, even as he waited for their knock and then opened the door.

'I'm Detective Sergeant Bradbury,' said the taller of the two. 'And this is Detective Constable Woods.'

They followed him in silence into the lounge, politely refused his offer of a drink and got down to business.

'Now sir,' said Bradbury, 'you came to us a couple of weeks ago telling us that your wife had, er, well, for want of a better word, gone.'

'Yes,' said George.

'So she went onto our Missing Persons File. Along with thousands of others.'

'Yes.'

'Why I'm telling you this', he said apologetically, conscious that George was still waiting to learn what they had come for, 'is because I don't want to upset you unnecessarily. Because, what's happened is there's been a woman's body found, unidentified, and our computer has produced a list of names of missing persons who it might be.' And he sat back in his chair, relieved at having come to the point.

'And it might be . . . Elaine,' said George, with the air of a man facing up to the worst.

'Probably not, but yes it could be.'

'I see.'

'So we're really here to try and rule out that possibility.'

George nodded. Everything they said reassured him in a way that they could never guess. They had obviously swallowed his story that Elaine had left him hook, line and sinker.

'The body, I should explain, was found yesterday on a beach in Devon. Drowned. Had been in the water for some time. We're not yet sure how long. Now, if you could give us a detailed description of your wife and, if possible, a recent photograph, we can then, I hope, eliminate her from our enquiries.'

Constable Woods flipped open his notebook and George obligingly told him Elaine's age, height, colouring and weight as near as he could remember it.

'And the colour of her eyes?'

'Blue.'

'And her hair?'

'Fair.'

'Did she have any other distinguishing characteristics?' asked the constable.

George could think of none. He could, of course, have filled both notebooks on the subject of her perverseness, her obstinacy, her arrogance and her selfishness but they were not the kind of characteristics easily recognizable in a corpse.

'No,' he said, 'not that I can think of.'

'Well, never mind,' said Bradbury, taking over again. 'I think we should have enough to go on. Now if you have a recent photograph . . . ?'

George left them in the room and went to search. There were the wedding pictures, of course, but he also recalled one that she had had taken just twelve months ago and been particularly proud of. He found it in the drawer of her dressing-table. It showed Elaine, wearing a bright green suit that had cost the earth, standing on the front lawn of the house. A breeze had tugged at her short hair, giving her a dashing appearance that had pleased her. 'I'm going to have it enlarged,' she had said, 'and then framed.' But she had done neither so now he was able to take it downstairs and give it to the sergeant.

'Thank you,' he said. 'We'll let you have it back as soon as possible.'

George went with them to their car, smiling in agreement at their comments on the size of the garden and the fact that they did not envy him the task of keeping on top of it. It was Constable Woods who noticed the green Mini.

'And whose car would that be, sir?' he asked.

'My wife's,' said George.

Both policemen went over and peered at it. Woods prodded with his foot at the deflated tyre.

'I can see why she didn't take it with her,' he said.

'Yes,' said George, and silently gave thanks for his own foresight.

'Oh, just one last thing,' said Bradbury. They were about to drive away and he had to lower the window of his car to speak to George. 'I don't know whether we've got it anyway but can you just tell us – what was the time and date on which you last saw your wife?'

It was so firmly relegated to the past that George had to think a moment.

'It was in the afternoon,' he said. 'I'm not sure what time exactly.'

'All right. And the date . . . ?'

'It was Saturday . . . Saturday, April twenty-sixth.'

The telephone rang ten minutes after the policeman had left.

'Hello,' said a voice that George did not immediately recognize.

'Yes?' he said.

'It's me. Josie.'

He responded with a little 'Ah!' of surprise but the full implication of her ringing him did not at first strike home. The visit of the police and the threat that it had brought with it had, temporarily at least, driven Josie from his mind. Now, as she spoke, she came back into it and he could picture her in her tight, black waitress uniform.

'You know that job that you said?'

'Yes,' he answered quickly. 'You mean as housekeeper?'

'That's it. Is it still going or what?'

He assured her that it was still going and waited with bated breath. This was indeed a bonus to the evening. He had started off nervous and tense, fearing arrest for murder, been reassured by the willingness of the police to look for his wife on a beach in Devon, and now here was Josie coming up trumps into the bargain.

'Well, when can I come then?' she said simply.

'As soon as you like.' It occurred to him that things ought to be done properly. 'Won't you have to give your notice first though?'

'No need. I got the sack this afternoon.'

So another piece of the jigsaw fell into place. She was ringing him in desperation. She had had to put aside the reservations about the job that he had detected in her when they had parted after the Admiral Lord Rodney. But why had she been sacked? He waited for her to offer the information but the silence between them lengthened. Finally, he had to ask.

'Why were you sacked?'

'He said I was fiddling the till. Which I wasn't. In actual fact it was because he was trying to get off with me and I wouldn't have any of it.'

She said it flatly, as if sure that he would not believe her. But he did. Immediately and without any doubts. There seemed nothing more natural to him than that anybody employing that seductive young lady should not sooner or later make a play for her.

'I see,' he said. 'Well, you can start here when you want.'

There was a pause.

'The trouble is', she said, 'I've got nowhere to sleep tonight now.'

Ten minutes later he was picking her up on the corner of Carlisle Street and Fenton Row. Two youths passing watched enviously as he dropped her canvas bag into the boot of his car. Josie herself stood sullenly, her hands thrust into her pockets. She seemed already uncertain about the wisdom of what she was letting herself in for and resentful of the fact that she had little choice.

'Jump in,' he said, and they were on their way to the White House.

It was an awkward evening. He led her to the guest room on the first floor with its prepared double bed. She stood at it without moving, suspicious and defensive.

'I'll leave you to unpack then,' he said.

'Yes.'

'Have you had anything to eat?'

She shook her head so he went down to the kitchen and busied himself preparing a steak and some ready-cut chips taken from the deep freeze. Ten minutes later she came down and sat on a stool watching him.

'Would you like a glass of wine with it?' he asked.

'No,' she replied abruptly – probably, he thought, wanting to keep her wits about her.

They talked about the job and what it would entail. Or rather he talked and she appeared to listen. He explained where things were kept and suggested a routine that she might follow. Part of the house, he acknowledged, needed renovation before it could be properly cleaned. She should not worry herself about that.

She finished the meal and, leaving him to the washing-up, went to bed early. He did not mind, knowing that he would have to play his part carefully if he was not to stampede her into an early departure. For the time being, he would be a conscientious employer, keeping their dealings on a strictly commercial basis. Later on, when she felt settled and at home, they might graduate to a more intimate relationship. But for a few days, or weeks even, he must do nothing to suggest that such a thought had ever crossed his mind.

In fact the next few days were so full of the unexpected that he had little time left for anything else, even for lusting after his new lodger.

First, the local paper came out with an article on the front page headed, 'Body That of Mortician's Wife?'. It carried all the information that the police had given George earlier about the body on the beach and reported their fears that it could turn out to be that of Mrs Elaine Webster, wife of George Webster, mortician at the Royal Infirmary. Following the appearance of the article came a rash of telephone calls from Elaine's friends who had read it and were falling over themselves to ring George with their condolences – even if such condolences were not yet strictly in order.

Eventually he left the phone off the hook, tired of the same conversation and irritated by the transparent motives of his enquirers. They had, he supposed cynically, enjoyed the scandal of Elaine's departure and were now doubly entertained to find that there might be more to come.

'That's about you in the paper, isn't it?' observed Josie.

She was still withdrawn and had gone about her first days of work in a lacklustre fashion.

'Yes,' he said.

'It says you're a mortician.'

'Yes.'

He would have been found out in his lie sooner or later anyway.

'What's one of them?' she asked.

He could not hide a smile. 'Oh, I'm in charge of a particular department. Covering everything to do with people who've died.'

This seemed to satisfy her.

The police arrived that same night, Sergeant Bradbury and Constable Woods again, though this time in a different car. They were bringing back the photograph and, with it, some news.

'I think we can reassure you, sir,' said Bradbury, looking much happier than he had on his previous visit. He even accepted George's offer of a cigarette. 'The post mortem has now been carried out and the findings have been published.' Then, as he realized, 'Well, of course, you'll know all about that, won't you, post mortems and so on. . . .'

'Well, something about it,' agreed George with a restrained smile.

'Only it seems that the body has been in the water for quite some time. At least a month. At least. Which would, of course, take us back beyond the time when you last saw your wife alive.'

'I'm glad to hear that,' said George.

'There are other variations in the description you gave us as well. But we needn't go into those since it's clear enough that, whoever it is, it can't be the body of your wife.'

'Wonderful,' said George. 'Will you join me in a drink?'

They accepted after a little show of reluctance and the conversation wandered to the house and what George planned to do with it.

Throughout all this Josie had not appeared. She was, he knew, somewhere about the premises. He supposed that she had witnessed the arrival of the policemen and, whether for reasons of her own or what, was keeping well out of the way.

However, the newspaper article and the police and the post mortem in Devon were no more than the beginning. Worse, much worse, was to follow. It came the following evening about six o'clock as George was reading the evening paper and Josie was in the kitchen preparing a meal.

It came in the shape of a tall young man with a southern accent who asked if he could speak to George on an important matter. He was extremely polite and seemed a touch nervous but what he had to say demolished George's feeling of security and left him in a state of panic and despair.

CHAPTER TWELVE

Martyn Culley went to see George Webster with great reluctance but knowing that it was the right thing to do.

He had been in Arncaster for four days when the local paper came out with its article headed 'Body That of Mortician's Wife?' He read it while alone in the house and having a leisurely, if sparse, breakfast. His hosts, Rob and Samantha, were out at work. Martyn's travels had brought him into contact with a variety of local newspapers and he enjoyed them with their intense detailing of local goings-on. The *Arncaster Mirror* was well up to standard, full of small scandals and minor controversies with columns of advertisements for everything under the sun. It was a jumble in the midst of which the mortician's wife seemed to have no particular significance.

Only later, as he was doing the washing-up, did a tiny detail come back to him from the article. Cirencester had been mentioned as her place of birth; she had come from there to Arncaster on her marriage to the mortician some three years ago.

'It can't be,' said Martyn aloud, struck by the enormity of the implications.

He went back to the paper, found the article and read it again, this time with a growing excitement. She was called Elaine Webster, was aged twenty-nine and had indeed been born in Cirencester.

She had disappeared on April twenty-sixth. He looked in his diary and calculated that the day on which he had been hitchhiking along the M4 and been picked up (and taken to a two-star hotel and seduced) had been May fifth – over a week later.

The name, of course, was wrong. The woman he had met had called herself Janet something-or-other, but then might not anyone wishing to stage a disappearance change their name as a matter of course anyway? She had certainly admitted to coming from Cirencester. She had just as certainly said that she had married a man from Arncaster and gone to live there.

Even more telling was the odd way in which she had referred to her husband's job.

'Actually, my husband deals in bodies,' was what she had said. 'But they don't run.'

It was the oddity of it that had lodged it in his memory. Then, when he had tried to guess at her husband's occupation – a doctor? chiropodist? P.E. instructor? – she had refused to tell.

Mortician was an answer that he would never have reached in a month of Sundays. Now it seemed so obvious that he became convinced in the instant that the woman he had met had been Elaine Webster, the missing wife of the mortician.

'Actually my husband deals in bodies. But they don't run.'

It was as plain as day. What was less clear was what the hell he should now do about it.

His fleeting love affair with Elaine – as he could now call her to himself – might have been what had brought him up the M1 and M6 to Arncaster but the thought of it had not much occupied him since he had arrived. There were forty or fifty thousand other people in Arncaster. The faint hope that he might bump into her became ridiculous the first morning that he strolled through the busy town centre.

Now that he had been reminded of her, he could almost feel her physical presence, as it had been when she was sitting beside him in the car, then lying beside him in the hotel bedroom. Part of him still longed to see her once more; though, of course, the newspaper article called into question whether anyone would ever do that again.

It also put him in something of a dilemma. There was a body in Devon that might or might not be hers. Investigations were proceeding to try and establish this. Much might turn, then, on when she was last seen alive. And he, Martyn, might well have been the last person to have done so, or at least the last to have seen her and then been made aware of her true identity. So he, and he alone, could step forward now and testify that Elaine Webster was alive and well a week after leaving her husband.

But should he do so? And, if so, then how?

He explained the problem to Rob that night. They had gone out to the Boot and Shoe for a drink.

'So what should I do? Find out where her husband lives and go and tell him or what?'

'But what have you got to tell him?'

'Well, just that I saw her alive on May fifth.'

He did not enlighten Rob as to the extent of his relationship with Elaine Webster.

Whether the lady was now alive or dead, he felt that to have boasted about his sexual conquest would have been unforgiveable.

'But what good's that?' asked Rob.

'Well, for one thing, it might help prove that she's not the body that they've found. And therefore that she's probably still alive.'

'Still be missing though, won't she.'

'Yes. But think about it from the husband's point of view, George Webster. He must be in agony till they find out whether it's her or not. And here am I, knowing something that might save him all that agony.'

Rob grunted and reached for his pint. He was a junior school teacher and seemed to have grown older and more tired since Martyn had last seen him. Samantha, his wife, had already complained to Martyn about his excessive drinking.

'And I wouldn't mind,' she said, 'but he does such stupid things when he's drunk!'

'Oh really,' said Martyn, not liking to ask what.

'He was nearly up in court six months ago for throwing a milk bottle at the town hall.'

Samantha, too, seemed older than Martyn remembered her, her face etched by lines of care. Or perhaps it was just that he himself, with his bohemian life-style, had remained unnaturally youthful so that his friends appeared aged in comparison. Samantha worked in a solicitor's office but had not yet qualified to be able to practise on her own. She and Rob had a modern, detached house on a new estate.

'Same again?' said Rob, leaving for the bar.

'No, I'm all right, thanks,' said Martyn. He disliked becoming drunk and was anyway wary of doing so in the company of someone who threw milk bottles at the town hall.

He would go and find George Webster and tell him what he knew. The more he thought about it, the more certain he became that that was the right thing to do. If Elaine were the body on the beach then at least he could offer some small consolation. Could tell her husband – and the police if necessary – that she had seemed well and happy on that wet afternoon that was now some two weeks ago. That might be important if a coroner's court were trying to decide between verdicts of suicide and accidental death. And if she were not the body on the beach, then his evidence – that he had seen her alive on May fifth – might help to eliminate that possibility early on and therefore shorten the unnecessary agonizing of her husband.

'One thing though,' said Rob, returning with his pint.

'What?'

'Suppose that you're wrong about the woman who gave you the lift? I mean suppose it wasn't his wife?'

Martyn had become so confident of this as to regard it as accepted fact. He now had to think for a moment to reassemble the clues that had convinced him.

'Well, then it would be the coincidence of the century,' he said. 'This woman I met was the right age. . . .'

Rob interrupted him. 'She told you her age?'

'Well, no. But she certainly *looked* the right age.'

'Go on.'

'She said that she lived in Arncaster. And when I commented that she hadn't got a northern accent she said that that was because she came from Cirencester but had three years ago married a man from Arncaster and gone to live there. There can't be two of them that've done that!'

'Why not?'

'Because it would be a ridiculous coincidence.'

'They happen.'

'Of course they happen. But in this case it woud be such a ridiculous coincidence that it's surely more sensible to assume that the woman I met was Elaine Webster and act on that assumption.'

His three years spent reading for a degree in philosophy had been admirable training. It might have left him jobless, but logical and moral dilemmas he could take in his stride.

'And remember what she said about his job,' he added, as Rob still seemed to have lingering doubts.

'What?'

'That he worked with bodies. But that they were bodies that didn't run.'

'She might have meant car bodies.'

Martyn laughed.

It was only much later, after closing time, when they were on their way home and crossing the canal that a further, disturbing possibility occurred to him. Suppose that the dead body on the beach were that of Elaine Webster – and that she had committed suicide in a fit of remorse and depression following their love-making?

The thought was so awful to him that he stopped and put out a hand to the stone parapet of the bridge as if for support.

'You all right?' said Rob, slurring his words.

'Yes,' said Martyn. 'Just something I've thought of, that's all.'

'It's this northern beer. Strong stuff if you're not used to it.'

It was this new interpretation of events that blunted Martyn's purpose the following morning. He had more or less decided to seek out George Webster as soon as possible and deliver his news: I have seen your wife. She gave me a lift along the M4 on the afternoon of May fifth. But now he hesitated. Suppose she had really died because of him?

Samantha was going in to work late so they had breakfast together. Rob, in black mood and hung-over, had thrown a pile of unmarked exercise books into his briefcase and gone.

'I don't know how he's going to end up,' said Samantha. 'But if he doesn't care, then I don't see why I should.'

She was wearing a rather flimsy dressing-gown, underneath

which she was naked. It struck Martyn that they should not perhaps be together in the house like this, particularly as she seemed so careless with the fastenings on her dressing-gown. He had not come here to help break up his friends' marriage.

Partly to distract her from any ideas she might have in that direction, he told her about his talk with Rob the night before.

'The trouble is,' he said, 'I'm still not sure what to do for the best.'

'Why not go to the police?' she suggested.

The honest answer would have been that he did not want the police to try and trace Elaine Webster's movements too closely. They might just succeed in discovering her name in the register of the Mitre Hotel in West London and receive a description of the tall, young man in wet denims accompanying her.

'I'd rather not,' he said vaguely. 'I thought of finding out where this George Webster lives and going to see him.'

'I'll tell you what,' she said. 'We do a lot of work with the police so I know some of them fairly well. I'll see if I can find out anything more about it, shall I?'

'Yes, all right then.'

His hesitation must have shown, for she added, 'Oh, don't worry. I can be discreet.'

It was only afterwards, when she had gone, that he wondered whether she had intended more by this. Had she been suggesting that if he fancied her then she could be discreet about that too?

She came back that evening with a photocopy of a photograph. It showed a woman standing on a lawn before a large house. The details had been blurred in the copying but it was a woman whom he recognized all the same. The short, blonde hair, the neat features, the slim figure, all reawakened a twinge that was at the same time one of longing and regret.

'That's his wife,' said Samantha.

It was also the woman who had given him a lift and with whom he had twice made love.

'How did you get it?' he asked, turning the photocopy over as if it might have more secrets to reveal.

'I told you we're pretty friendly with the police. They'd got the original from her husband and I got them to make me a copy.'

Seeing the picture had made his mind up. The slight doubt as to her identity had been his excuse for stalling. He now had to seek out George Webster and tell him what he knew. It was his clear duty and one that he must not shirk any longer.

'Had a good day, you two?' said Rob, coming in and throwing his briefcase into a corner.

'Yes, thanks,' said Martyn. 'Have you?'

'Foul,' said Rob.

Martyn explained to them over dinner what he now intended to do and they discussed how he might best track down George Webster.

'Ring the hospital,' suggested Rob, 'and ask for the mortuary. At least you know that that's where he works.'

'He won't be there now though, surely,' objected Samantha.

'I suppose not, no, but they'll have his address.'

'They might have it but I'm sure they won't tell Martyn what it is.'

'Why not?'

'No hospital will give out the home addresses of their staff to somebody asking over the phone,' she said firmly.

In the event it could not have been easier. They looked in the phone book and there it was: George Webster. The White House. Old Moore's Hill. Arncaster. Arncaster 32794.

'Unusual address,' said Samantha. 'Doesn't sound like your average terrace.'

As soon as dinner was over, Martyn shut himself in the hall with the telephone. He sat on the bottom step of the staircase with the directory on his knee and dialled the number.

It was seven rings before anyone answered and then, unexpectedly, it was a woman's voice – or perhaps a girl's.

'Yeah?'

'Oh hello. Is that Arncaster 32794?'

'Yeah.'

'Could I speak to George Webster, please?'

'Hang on. I'll tell him.'

There was a bang as the receiver was put down. He could hear footsteps going away and wondered who he had been speaking to. Probably a daughter, though, since George Webster had been married to Elaine Webster for only three years, it would have to be a daughter from a former marriage.

'George Webster here.'

'Oh hello. I wonder if I could see you regarding an important matter. It's something that I'd rather not discuss over the phone.'

It was a little speech that he had planned and silently rehearsed, aware of the difficulty he would have in making clear who he was and what he wanted. He was also conscious of how easily he might hurt the man's feelings or alarm him by announcing boldly that he wanted to talk to him about his missing wife.

George Webster sounded understandably puzzled. 'But what is it about?'

'Well, as I say, it's something that I'd rather not talk about over the telephone.'

'Who are you?'

'My name's Martyn Culley. But you don't know me. We've never met.'

There was a pause, then a reluctant agreement. 'Oh, all right then. Well, do you want to come up here to the house?'

'Well, if you don't mind, yes.'

And they agreed that Martyn would be there in about half an hour.

Samantha gave him directions and Rob offered either to drive him or lend him his car.

'No point in taking up your time,' said Martyn. 'I'll find it all right.'

In point of fact it was a journey that he wanted to make alone. He was not relishing the prospect of meeting this man and knew that he would feel guilty in his presence. Things would be awkward enough without Rob there as a witness.

'Here you are then,' said Rob, and threw him the car keys. 'If I'm not here when you get back I'll be in the pub. Come and tell me how you get on.'

CHAPTER THIRTEEN

'So. What was it you wanted to see me about?'

They were in the lounge of the White House, which had turned out to be every bit as imposing as its name had suggested. Martyn was sitting in the armchair to which he had been shown. He felt ill-at-ease, knowing that the story that he was about to tell was dishonest – not in what it said but in what it left out. George Webster, a thin, anxious-looking man of slightly less than average height, was standing some distance away.

Martyn took a deep breath. 'It's about your wife.'

The surprise and concern showed immediately on George Webster's face, as Martyn had feared that it would. He hurried on. 'It's just that I think I saw her and talked to her something over a week ago. I think she was a lady who stopped and gave me a lift when I was hitch-hiking to London.'

George Webster said nothing. He stared at Martyn as if there was something that he had not understood.

'Of course I didn't realize who she was till I read the article in this week's *Arncaster Mirror*. And then I thought I should come and tell you.'

'When was this?' said George Webster finally.

'When I met her?'

'Yes.'

'May the fifth.'

Another pause. And another suspicious look. It was clear that, for whatever reason, George Webster did not believe him.

'How did you know that she was my wife?'

Martyn eagerly recited the evidence: that she had been born in

106

Cirencester, had married a man from Arncaster and moved there three years ago, and the cryptic reference to his profession. 'And then I saw the article. And suddenly it all made sense.'

'Did she tell you her name?'

'Well, yes. But not Elaine Webster. She said that she was called Janet. Janet Megson I think it was. But with everything else pointing to her being your wife I thought that she must have made up a false name for some reason or other.'

'I see.'

'And since then I've seen her photograph.'

'A photograph of my wife?'

'Yes.'

'Where?'

'It's one the police had. I think it must have been taken outside this house. With her standing on the lawn.'

George nodded slowly as if forced to accept the truth of this against his will; then he shot Martyn another question.

'And you recognized her?'

'Oh yes.'

'The woman in the photograph was the woman who had given you a lift and told you these things about herself?'

'Definitely.'

'On May fifth?'

'Yes.'

They were interrupted by the arrival of the coffee that Martyn had been offered and accepted when he had first arrived. It was brought in by a girl who must have been the person that he had first spoken to on the telephone. She was attractive, or anyway sexy, with a tee-shirt and jeans combination that did full justice to her figure.

She put the tray down on a table, leaving George Webster to collect his own cup while she brought Martyn's across to him.

'You said no sugar.'

'Yes. Thank you.'

She gave him a little smile that was touched with curiosity. But it was a smile that switched off when she turned to George Webster. 'Anything else?'

107

'Er, no. No, thank you,' he said.

She left the room, though not before she had glanced again at Martyn and repeated the little, inviting smile.

The interruption seemed to have given George Webster time to have come to terms with what Martyn had told him.

'Well,' he said in a tone that was less hostile, more conciliatory, 'it does sound like my wife, I must admit.'

'It's just that I thought I should come and tell you. After what I'd read in the newspaper. I mean in case it . . . has any bearing on things.'

'Oh, you mean on whether that body that they've found could be her.'

'Well, yes,' said Martyn, relieved that they had at last come to the heart of the matter.

'Oh, but that's all been cleared up,' said George Webster. 'It couldn't be her anyway.'

Martyn looked at him in surprise. 'Oh. Oh, well, I'm, er, I'm glad to hear that.'

'The body had been in the water for too long. Even working from the date when I last saw her – April twenty sixth – it couldn't have been her.'

This was good news indeed. It meant that all Martyn's fears that he might have unwittingly helped to push Elaine Webster towards suicide were unfounded. She had not been stricken with remorse after their amorous encounter. He had nothing to reproach himself with on that score, though he still felt uneasy in the presence of her husband. He was, after all, still a fraud, posing as the bringer of good news to a man with whose wife he had slept.

'I don't know that there's much more that I can tell you about her,' he said.

'No,' said George Webster. 'Well, after all, if she only gave you a lift. . . .'

'Yes.'

There was a pause as they sipped at their coffees. Martyn allowed himself a glance round the opulently furnished room. It seemed an unusual setting for a mortician. But he was being asked a question.

'So you don't live in Arncaster then?'

'No. I'm just here visiting friends.' And he told George Webster about his wandering life-style since he had left university. Unable to talk freely about the other man's wife, he could at least do so about himself.

George Webster seemed interested. 'So you've no regular job?'

'No.' Martyn gave an apologetic little laugh. 'I keep thinking I must get one sooner or later but I haven't managed it so far.'

'So what do you do for money?'

The question was unexpectedly direct but Martyn did not mind.

'Oh, I get some social security. And I sometimes get temporary jobs here and there.'

George Webster nodded. He was staring at Martyn again so that Martyn searched his mind for something further to say. It seemed that something was called for, was expected, but for the life of him Martyn could not think what it was and the moment passed.

'Well, thank you for coming.'

This was his cue to leave. They walked together out into the garden. He caught a glimpse of the girl watching through the half-open kitchen door as they went and wondered if she was, after all, Webster's daughter. Something in their attitudes to each other suggested otherwise.

'It's an amazing house,' said Martyn politely as they walked to his car. He had parked it beside a green Mini on the front drive.

'Still needs a lot doing to it.'

'Yes, I'm sure.'

The garden was unkempt for a start. Someone had made an effort here and there but the main part behind and to the side of the house looked only one remove from a wilderness.

'I wonder,' said George Webster, 'if you have a phone number where I might contact you. In case anything comes up.'

'Yes, of course,' said Martyn, and gave him Rob and Samantha's home number which he copied down on the back of a cigarette packet. 'Though I might not be there for very long.'

'You might be off on your travels again?'

'Yes. I should try and find a job actually. Get some money together.'

109

This drew another quick stare from George Webster. There was still, Martyn felt, some misunderstanding between them but he had no idea what it could be.

'Well,' he said, 'I hope everything turns out all right.'

'Thank you.'

They shook hands. Martyn got into his borrowed car and drove away. Coming to the gates, before the steep descent began, he caught sight of George Webster in the wing-mirror. He was standing watching him go, framed by the house in the same way that his wife had been in the photograph that Samantha had brought from the police.

Rob was not at home so Martyn caught up with him in the pub where he was already onto his second pint.

'Well. And how did it go then?'

Martyn gave him a run-down on the visit and began to realize, as he did so, how strange it had all been.

'He was older than I'd expected – certainly older than she was. Or rather than she *is*. Like I say, that body wasn't her at all.'

'Pleased to hear about her, was he?'

'Well, not. . . .' Martyn hesitated. No, George Webster had not been pleased. He had been puzzled and he had been suspicious but he had certainly not been pleased. Even when he had eventually come to accept the truth of Martyn's story he had shown little curiosity about what Martyn might have been able to tell him about his missing wife. What sort of mood had she been in? Where was she coming from when she gave him a lift? Where was she on her way to? All questions that Martyn would have been happy enough to have tried to answer had they ever been asked. 'No, he didn't seem too bothered to tell you the truth.'

Though even that was not entirely true. The man had certainly been bothered; had been worried and, if anything, more ill-at-ease with Martyn than Martyn had been with him.

'Maybe he was glad to see her go,' said Rob. 'Another pint?'

'A half please.'

Perhaps he had indeed been glad to see her go. Perhaps her habit of seducing hitch-hikers was one that he knew all about and with which he could no longer live.

'He's there on his own now then, is he?' asked Rob, coming back with the drinks.

'No.' And this had been another strange little ingredient in the evening's visit. 'No, there's a girl there as well.'

Rob laughed. 'No wonder he didn't want to hear from you about his wife then!'

That made sense of a kind. Perhaps the girl had been the cause of the wife's leaving. Perhaps Elaine Webster had marched out in high dudgeon after catching the two of them together. And perhaps her seduction of Martyn had an element of revenge to it.

It was a strange scenario, but he could think of no other to explain the man's almost total lack of curiosity as to his wife's state of mind and whereabouts. He had seemed much more interested in Martyn himself, why he travelled as he did and what he did for money.

'By the way,' said Martyn, 'I gave him your telephone number. He asked if I had somewhere where I could be contacted.'

'Yes, that's all right. But what would he want to contact you for?'

'I don't know.' It was a fair question though, just another little oddity to add to those that Martyn had not noticed at the time. 'I suppose it's in case he thinks of anything else that he wants to ask me.'

CHAPTER FOURTEEN

The following morning Martyn was faintly alarmed to find that Samantha was again late in leaving for work. Rob had already disappeared when she joined Martyn at the table in her dressing-gown.

'You found your mortician last night then?'

'Yes.' And, glad to have something to talk about, he gave her a potted history of the meeting. The strangeness of George Webster's attitude, which had so puzzled him the previous night, seemed less peculiar in the light of day. Perhaps he had accepted the finality of his wife's departure and was no longer interested in hearing about what she might be up to now – after all, she had deserted him. Or perhaps he had been so taken aback by Martyn's arrival that he had not had time to think of those questions that he would like to ask.

'I forgot to tell you,' said Samantha, eating a piece of toast, 'what my tame policeman told me about your Mrs Webster.'

'What?'

'Oh, apparently she took a load of money with her when she went. Just collected a load of cash and then vamoosed. And that she had a lover.'

It was information that he could have done without. Not, of course, that he was jealous. That was absurd. He had known her for only one afternoon.

'Oh?' he said, apparently unconcerned.

'I mean a lover here in Arncaster. Though, according to my policeman, she's left him behind as well as her husband.'

It was disappointment more than anything else. Having known

and loved her for a while, he was disappointed that she should have behaved so badly. She had not left, as he had first suspected, because of her husband's infidelities, but had practised infidelities of her own and then coolly walked out with a handbag full of loot. He remembered the calm way in which she had handled the business of signing them in at the hotel.

'He's probably better off without her then,' he said lightly.

'Sounds like it.'

She had finished her toast and cup of coffee and stood up from the table. She gave a small yawn and stretched, her arms up above her head. Martyn realized with a shock that, silhouetted as she was against the window, he could see her naked body through the thin material of her dressing-gown. He looked quickly down at his folded copy of *The Guardian*.

'I'm going to have a shower,' she said. 'You coming?'

It might have been a joke and he was keen to take it as one.

'No thanks,' he said, and tried for a joke of his own. 'I get claustrophobic with other people in showers.'

But she knew a rejection when she heard one and was not entertained by it.

'Suit yourself,' she said coldly, and left the room.

He gave a sigh of annoyance. Now he would have to leave, and quickly. She had risked exposing herself to him – in more ways than one – and must now hate him for his refusal to play along. Not that he found her unattractive. His body had responded to the view of her stretched figure even as he had been determined to ignore the offer. She was, first and foremost, the wife of his friend. And the last thing he wanted to do was to repay the hospitality that had been given him by becoming involved in a marriage that seemed to have its share of problems even without him. Besides which, his talk with George Webster was still fresh in his mind. The complications that had followed a sexual encounter which had taken place 250 miles away was a warning to him of what might follow a shower with Samantha.

Women had always found him attractive. He had a fine physique and an almost old-fashioned handsomeness that had placed him ahead of the field from an early age. What they seemed less able to accept was his right to say no to them because they happened to be, say, married to another man.

Samantha put her head round the door.

'I'm going,' she said. Then added tartly, 'So you're safe now.'

'Have a nice day,' he said apologetically, and heard the door slam as she left.

He would depart the following morning. To set out there and then without a word to Rob would have been discourteous and, anyway, might have seemed suspicious. He would spend the day looking for jobs and finding a new destination.

There was an advertisement in *The Guardian* for a trainee theatre administrator that caught his fancy. It was at least one of the few remaining areas of employment in which he had not already tried and failed. He went out to the nearest newsagent, bought a note-pad and some envelopes, came back and wrote his customary letter of application. Posting it, he then went on to the library reading-room. The *New Statesman*, *Punch*, *Lancashire Life*, they were all there but their jobs vacant columns were meagre and offered nothing for which he could apply with even the slightest hope of success.

His outing to the pub with Rob that evening confirmed the wisdom of his decision to leave.

They had gone to the Boot and Shoe. Rob entertained him with stories of anarchy in the classroom then, as drink loosened his tongue, began to talk about Samantha.

'I know that she has a bit on the side. She thinks I don't but I'd have to be bloody stupid not to.'

'How is she finding her job?' asked Martyn, desperate to forestall such confessions. He knew from experience that few friendships survived such intimacies recounted after four pints and were sure to be bitterly regretted the next day.

'Never mind her job,' insisted Rob. 'It's not her job that I've got to worry about.'

'I'm sure you haven't got anything to worry about.'

'Oh no?'

'You always made the perfect pair,' urged Martyn as best he could. 'Even at university, and there weren't many there stayed together for longer than a month or two.'

For a moment Rob seemed willing to be distracted. 'No, well, you certainly didn't anyway.'

'Oh, me. . . .'

'You must have got through more birds at that university than most of us had hot dinners.'

Martyn smiled and shrugged. It was not that he had wished to be a philanderer, just that, after the first few idyllic weeks of afternoon sex and pop concerts, his partners seemed to sense his lack of commitment and drifted away. He let them go, never doubting their right to do as they wished.

But Rob's mind returned to his wife. He leaned forward confidentially and gripped Martyn's wrist.

'Listen. I don't mind if, you know, you and Samantha have been having it away on the quiet.'

'Oh, come on!' protested Martyn. He was relieved to hear shouts of 'Time!' and 'Let's have your glasses!' in the background.

'No, I know what she's like. I wouldn't blame you. I mean I'd probably do the same myself in your situation.'

'There's been nothing between me and Samantha,' said Martyn firmly.

Rob shrugged. Clearly he did not believe him and never would.

A man came round collecting glasses. 'Come on now. It's after time.'

'You talking to me?' said Rob, rising aggressively.

Martyn had to stand and put a restraining hand on his friend's shoulder. 'Come on. Time we were off.'

For a moment Rob looked ready to take on not only the barman but Martyn as well, then satisfied himself by shouting, 'Glad to get out of this bloody place!' at the barman and allowed Martyn to lead him to the door.

Samantha was in bed – mercifully so – when they arrived back at the house. Martyn refused Rob's invitation to join him in a nightcap and went upstairs to the spare room. He set the alarm on his watch for seven o'clock, planning to make his getaway before Rob and Samantha were even awake. Still with no real destination, he would return first to his friends in Hammersmith, then see what

115

life had to offer.

'Good night everybody,' sang out Rob, going past the door. 'Sweet dreams!'

Seven-and-a-half hours later Martyn was awake and padding around the silent house. He snatched a cup of coffee, packed his rucksack, took a sheet of writing-paper and wrote, 'Thanks for everything. Must keep in touch. Cheers. Martyn,' and stuck it under the flap of Rob's briefcase.

He was at the front door and noiselessly opening the latch when the telephone began to ring.

For a moment he thought of ignoring it but he had never done so before and could not start now. He went back and picked up the receiver.

'Hello?' he said, and read the number from the phone's circular disc, 'Arncaster 33865.'

To his surprise it was for him.

'Martyn Culley?'

'Yes.'

'It's George Webster here.' For a moment Martyn could not think of a reply. 'You came to see me the other night.'

'Oh, I remember, yes.'

'I wonder if I could see you again. Just for a short chat. If it's convenient.'

It was hardly that; not when Martyn was standing with a rucksack over one shoulder and had been about to leg it for the M6. But he felt in debt to George Webster; he had done him a wrong in making love to his wife; staying now would be a small act of atonement. He let the rucksack slide down onto the carpet.

'Yes, all right then,' he said. 'Whenever you like.'

There was a shout from upstairs – 'Is that for me?' from Samantha. Martyn put a hand over the receiver and called back – 'No, it's for me.' This seemed to give George Webster time to sort things out.

'I'm going to work,' he said, 'and I'll be there from nine till five-thirty. You could always come there. Or else it'll have to wait till I'm home this evening.'

'I'll come and see you this morning,' said Martyn, thinking of

116

minimizing the delay to his journey. They agreed that he would be at the mortuary for ten o'clock.

The hospital could not be missed, its sprawling complex dominating the eastern edge of the town. The mortuary was signposted along with a myriad of other departments.

George Webster had opened the door to him before he had had time to push the bell marked 'Ring for attention'. He was dressed in a white smock and, from the start, seemed more at home and friendlier than he had done in his own home two nights ago.

'We can talk in here,' he said, ushering Martyn into an office. A younger man, also dressed in white and carrying an armful of wreaths, went past them.

'I'll not be long, Kevin,' George Webster called. 'And Mr Charlesworth won't be here for at least an hour.'

Martyn sat on a rather rickety chair and the door was closed.

'Cup of tea?'

'Er, yes please.'

George busied himself with an electric kettle and some tea-bags.

'It's nice of you to come,' he said, 'and I'm sorry if I didn't seem very welcoming the other night.' Martyn started to object but he went on, 'It's just that you caught me a bit by surprise, that was all. It's been a difficult time for me these last few weeks.'

'I'm sure it must have been,' muttered Martyn. Samantha's account of Elaine Webster's departure had made it clear where the blame lay and had awakened Martyn's sympathies towards the mortician.

Once the tea was ready, Martyn prepared himself to chat about his meeting with Elaine, regretting that he could still not be completely honest about it. But, to his surprise, he found that George had something else that he wanted to talk about.

'I was thinking about you needing a job.'

'Oh,' said Martyn in surprise.

'You are still looking for one?'

'Yes.'

'Well, I certainly have a lot of work that needs doing. I just wondered, if you were at a loose end, whether you might like to come and stay at the house and help me with the garden and one or

117

two other things.'

Martyn's first impulse was one of polite refusal. He had determined on leaving the town and would have already been well on his way but for the last-second phone call. But it seemed an ungrateful response. George Webster had problems enough of his own yet had had time to be concerned about Martyn's lack of a job. Looking back, the questions he had asked the other night – about Martyn's way of life and what he did for money – were not so strange after all. They were those of a man naturally sympathetic to those with whom he came into contact. How deeply he must have felt the betrayal of his wife.

'Well, it's very kind of you,' said Martyn, still uncertain.

'You're a strong-looking young chap. I'm sure you'll enjoy it, a bit of gardening, a spot of redecorating, according to the weather. For just as long as you like.'

The physical labour would be a welcome change certainly. And he would be away from Rob and Samantha, which was his only reason for wanting to go away immediately from Arncaster.

'£50 a week and your board and lodging. How would that suit you?'

As Martyn considered, George Webster watched him, nervously turning a cigarette over and over in his fingers. It seemed important to him that Martyn should accept. Perhaps he felt a bond between them after Martyn's encounter with his missing wife.

'All right then,' said Martyn. 'It's a deal.'

'Good.'

'Just for a week or two anyway.'

'Oh yes. For just as long as you like.'

As they finished their tea, George outlined some of the work that needed doing: grass-cutting, tree-pruning, the removal of old rubble, then miles of paintwork to be cleaned and restored.

'I'll run you up there now,' he said, glancing at his watch. 'Then you can get yourself settled in.'

Martyn agreed and they left the office. In a large, gloomy room lined by what looked like huge refrigerators, the young man called Kevin was sitting reading a magazine.

'I'll be back in about twenty minutes,' George told him.

'Suppose Mr Charlesworth wants to start early?'

George hesitated. 'Well look, if we take the body in there now, you could make a start on your own if need be, couldn't you?'

'Definitely,' replied Kevin. He seemed pleased at the prospect.

George first led Martyn outside into the sunshine.

'Sorry, but I can't let you see this,' he explained. 'A body's entitled to its privacy, even though it is dead.'

'Of course,' agreed Martyn, who was glad to get out of the chilly atmosphere of the mortuary.

'Shan't be long.'

Left alone outside and the time to think, Martyn saw the first possible flaw in the arrangement. Suppose that Elaine Webster should return? Suppose that she should come back to her husband, full of remorse and wanting to start again – only to find in residence the young man to whom she had given a lift and then so much more? The prospect so alarmed him that he was tempted to change his mind and hitch back to London as he had intended all along.

Till he considered the odds. The Elaine Webster that he had met and since heard about was unlikely ever to return. And – in the unlikely event that she should while he was there – she was clearly a cool enough cookie to brazen things out till he could make his getaway.

George hurried out ten minutes later, now without his white smock. They got into his car, which was a white Volvo estate, and drove across the town. It was a town that Martyn now felt he was coming to know.

'By the way,' said George as he drove, 'something you said the other night I found a bit odd.'

'What was that?'

'Just the question of when it was exactly that you met Elaine – my wife.'

'What time of day?'

'No, the date. What date was it that you said?'

'Well, I wasn't sure myself until I'd looked in my diary,' said Martyn, eager to be helpful. 'It was the day that I left my parents' place. I'd been staying there for a couple of weeks. And it was just three days before I had an interview with British Airways.'

'And what date was that?'

'May the fifth. Friday, May fifth. See, my interview was on Monday, May the eighth.'

There was a silence. They were climbing out of the town now, up the winding hill that led to the White House at the top.

'If you don't mind my asking,' said Martyn, 'why should that be odd?'

But George became flustered and Martyn wished that he had not asked. 'Oh, just something. . . . Nothing for you to worry about. . . .'

They were approaching the dilapidated gates with the three-storey house showing just beyond them before George explained about Josie.

'The girl who brought the coffee in the other night.'

'Yes,' said Martyn. 'I remember her.'

'Well, she also works for me. And lives in. She's a sort of housekeeper. Been helping out since my wife went.'

It seemed an unusual job for a young girl but Martyn had no reason to doubt the explanation. He knew better than most the difficulties of finding any job at all.

The girl called Josie was there waiting when they went into the house. She gazed at Martyn with an undisguised curiosity.

'Be nice to have a bit of company out here,' she said when George introduced them.

'Well, I don't know just how long I'll be here for,' Martyn answered wth a little laugh. When George had talked to him about gardening and decorating he had not expected it to involve being thrown together with a curvaceous young lady in tight jeans. She was, he guessed, in her late teens.

'I'd better be getting back,' said George. Then to Josie, 'You can show Martyn round, can't you?'

'Yeah,' she said in the same off-hand fashion that she had used to address him before. 'Why not.'

And he left them together in the kitchen.

'Well,' said Josie, barely waiting for him to be out of earshot, 'he's got you here as well then, has he?'

'He wanted somebody to do some gardening and I happened to

120

be around,' replied Martyn evasively. He did not want to be drawn into a conspiracy between the two of them against George.

'He said you were a student.'

'Well, I used to be,' said Martyn, with a little laugh. 'Haven't found anything else to be since, that's all.'

She had gone back to her task of peeling potatoes. 'I'll show you round when I've finished this, OK?'

Martyn suggested that, until she was ready, he might have a stroll around on his own.

'Do what you like,' she said. 'But be careful. There's all sorts goes on here.'

He looked at her but she did not elaborate. Presumably it was some kind of joke.

He went outside and walked round, past the garage and the outbuildings, to the back of the house which he had not previously seen. The garden seemed to stretch forever. He took a kick at the long grass, looking forward to the challenge of taming it. Once again fate had provided him with a purpose in life and he was happy to accept it until another came along.

It seemed an odd *ménage à trois* but none the worse for that. As his stay with Rob and Samantha had demonstrated, it was often the conventional-seeming households that were the most dangerous. He would set out to enjoy his stay here, treating it as a working holiday.

CHAPTER FIFTEEN

They were in bed together by three o'clock that same afternoon. Martyn, new to the house, was not even sure just whose bed it was.

As he had wandered about the grounds, Josie had made them a lunch of defrosted pizzas and then surprised him by producing a bottle of white wine from the top shelf of the pantry.

'Won't Mr Webster mind?' Martyn had hesitantly enquired on being presented with the bottle and a corkscrew.

Josie had laughed. 'George, you mean? No, he won't mind! Says I can help meself to anything!'

Afterwards she had become seductive in a heavy-handed fashion.

'What shall we do now then?'

'Well,' said Martyn, though well aware of the implied invitation, 'I thought I might make a start on the garden.'

'Oh, not yet. You don't have to start this afternoon!'

'Might as well,' said Martyn. 'I've nothing else to do.'

This produced a grin from her. 'I'm sure we can find something.'

Her uninhibited approach was infectious. He could not help returning her grin and thereby admitting that he knew what she had in mind.

Would there, though, be unforeseen complications here as there had been following his last sexual encounter, with Elaine Webster at the end of the M4? His brain, made lazy by the wine, flicked through the possibilities: that Josie was already George Webster's lover (highly unlikely), that she was secretly married to someone else altogether (no chance), or that George might come back and find them together.

'He never gets back before half-five,' she said as though reading his thoughts.

She came round the table towards him and stood provocatively, within touching distance, waiting.

Martyn's resistance ebbed away. There was no-one else's marriage to be considered here, just a randy young lady who had made free with her employer's wine and would now do the same with his beds. And who – he finally admitted to himself – he liked and found attractive. He reached out and gently pulled her to him. She came eagerly and locked her mouth onto his before he could rise from the kitchen chair.

Sex in the afternoon brought back nostalgic memories of university. It had been a communal life that had encouraged the easy swapping of partners. Arts students in particular had had a light timetable with frequent gaps between lectures and seminars that needed filling by some activity that was both cheap and intellectually undemanding.

'Don't you think he's creepy?' asked Josie after they had finished and were lying apart in the brass bed in what, looking round, Martyn took to be some sort of guest room.

'Who?'

'George.'

'Well,' said Martyn, 'he's been very kind to me. And, let's face it, he has had a difficult time.'

'He never liked her. I think he's glad she's gone.' And when Martyn hesitated to agree she added, 'He was trying to get off with me even before she went.'

Martyn contented himself with a slight grunt, not wanting to seem interested in case he would be offered some new insight that would turn the situation on its head. And he felt honour-bound to resist any kind of conspiracy with Josie against their employer. It would be a poor way of returning his generosity.

'You'll be sleeping in here,' said Josie, ending the mystery of just whose room they were in.

'Oh. Very nice,' said Martyn, looking round with a new interest. It was a large room that Elaine's schemes for redecoration had not reached. There was a flowered wallpaper, made faint by age, and an old-fashioned, cracked wash-basin in one corner.

'I'd keep your door locked as well if I was you,' she giggled.

He played along with her. 'Why? In case you come molesting me in the middle of the night?'

But, surprisingly, that had not been the suggestion.

'Oh, I didn't mean that,' she said. 'Though I might do now that you mention it.'

'What did you mean then?' yawned Martyn.

'Oh, you'd be surprised. I told you, it's a funny house is this.' And, before he could enquire further, she had swung herself out of bed and was padding, naked, towards the door. 'Be back in a minute. I've left my fags downstairs.'

She disappeared, leaving him to wonder what she meant, and to decide that it was probably nothing. Having been a few days in the house before him, she wanted to impress and intrigue him by hinting at a superior knowledge of its ways.

George came home at half-five as she had predicted and for the first time, as he relaxed in the lounge, Martyn had the chance of a chat with him that had no specific purpose. He decided to ask him about his job.

'Does it affect the way you think about people?'

'How do you mean?'

'I mean having to deal with dead bodies all the time. Does it affect your attitude towards living people?'

George gave him a look that revealed again the suspicion and defensiveness that had marked their first meeting. Perhaps the rites of the mortician were regarded as secretive and not to be asked about.

'No,' came the abrupt reply.

'I don't mean in any strange way,' said Martyn apologetically. 'I just wondered if it affected your view of their spiritual or religious nature.'

George looked at him again. He still seemed puzzled, either by the question or by Martyn's motives in asking it.

Martyn tried again. 'Does it make you think any less of human life?' It was not quite what he meant but George's lack of response was pushing him towards wild simplifications of the point he had first intended.

'Make me think less of it . . . ?' echoed George, now clearly displeased.

Martyn sighed and began again. 'What I mean is. . . .' But George had heard enough and stopped him.

'You mean do I think human life matters? Well, I do, yes. The people I cut up are dead, you know!' And, openly hostile, he got up from his chair, gave another bitter look at the astonished Martyn, and left the room.

Martyn had no option but to let him go. He knew that his question had been awkwardly put but still could not understand the antagonism that it had provoked. It was clearly a subject best left alone. He must try and repair the damage to their relationship.

Fortunately, George seemed to have made the same resolution so that when they met again over dinner there was almost an excess of politeness and concern on both sides. Josie, too, was in a playful mood and showed none of her earlier sullenness towards George. Martyn, in fact, worried slightly that George might put two and two together, noticing this change in her and how it had coincided with Martyn's own arrival, but he showed no signs of doing so.

The next few days stayed warm and grew warmer so that Martyn was able to work exclusively on the garden. He worked without a shirt and, as the sun came out and stayed there, he even began to show a light tan. He was also able to show a rapid improvement in the state of the garden. getting a real kick out of the progress that each day achieved. The novelty of outdoor physical work was exhilarating.

'Don't overdo it,' warned George, coming home late one evening to find Martyn still working away. 'It's been like this for long enough. There's no rush to get things straight.'

'Don't worry,' grinned Martyn from his perch halfway up a crab-apple tree from which he was trimming the dead branches, 'I'm enjoying it!'

For much of the time Josie came out and sunbathed near him, leaving the house to grow dusty as it pleased. She had no swimming-costume so unceremoniously peeled off her clothes and lay there naked.

'Supposing somebody comes?' said Martyn, momentarily distracted from his work.

'Nobody will. Not out here!'

'Well, what about me then?' he protested weakly. 'How am I to concentrate on cutting grass?'

'**Don**'t look,' she said, pleased at the effect she was having.

He tried not to, patiently applying himself to cutting the grass and brambles and then carting them by wheelbarrow to the growing pile at the back of the house. But she was always there, in the corner of his eye, chewing on a spike of grass or painting and re-painting her finger- and toe-nails bright red. Sooner or later, each morning and each afternoon, they would end up retiring to the cool of his bedroom.

He pointed out that he was being paid for working in the garden, not for indulging in sexual high jinks.

'Think of it as being instead of a tea-break,' she said.

It was something of a relief when a swarm of midges seemed to find her flesh as sweet as he did and came to find her whenever she emerged. 'Blasted things!' she said, slapping at them, but finally admitting defeat and retiring indoors.

She came out later, keeping her clothes on, and sat on a low wall near the flower-bed that he was digging over. It might have been that she felt the need to come up with a new way of distracting him and reclaiming his attention. Anyway, she returned to her theme of the mystery of the house.

'Don't you want to know what it is?'

'If you want to tell me.'

She sat chewing for a while, building the tension, then said, 'There's a ghost.'

He laughed. 'What, in this house?'

'Yes!'

He laughed again. He could not help it. His deepest beliefs were in rationality and logic and left little room for such fancies.

'There is!' she insisted, put out by his amusement.

'And have you seen it?' he said teasingly.

'Plenty of people have,' she said, avoiding the question.

'Who?'

It entertained him that they should have something to argue over as he worked, a diverting bone of contention. The few days that he had spent isolated with Josie had been remarkable more for their physical than their intellectual stimulation.

'Oh, lots of people! That old farmer-woman who brings the milk for one.'

'And she told you about it?'

'Yes.'

'Well, go on then. What kind of ghost is it? An old man with a ball and chain clanking after him?'

'No. A woman. She has a grey dress on and she's reading a Bible.'

'Why a Bible? Don't tell me it's because she's scared of ghosts!' joked Martyn.

'Oh, all right, be clever about it,' said Josie, annoyed. She turned her back to him, picked up a handful of stones and began throwing them one by one at the sundial.

Sorry that he had annoyed her, Martyn tried to respond with the seriousness that she wanted. 'No, I would like to know. Really.' The stone-throwing stopped. 'Did the milk lady tell you anything about her history?'

Josie turned back to him, mollified and eager to relate the story. 'She told me that the ghost was the mistress of the man who used to live here. And that the man's wife had found out what was going on and had poisoned her. And that she'd come back to haunt the wife!'

'When was this?'

'Oh, a long time ago,' said Josie vaguely.

'This century?'

'I don't know,' she admitted. Then added, 'What I thought was, whether his wife – Elaine or whatever she was called – had seen this ghost and that was why she ran off.' And she waited to receive Martyn's verdict on her little piece of deduction.

'Could be,' he said, not wanting to annoy her again.

'I'll tell you what though,' she said.

'What?'

'I'm glad that I've never had anything to do with him.'

'With George?' said Martyn, not following.

'Yes. I mean, you know, not been his mistress or anything. Or else I'd be in the same position as that ghost woman was wouldn't I?'

Martyn felt that the parallel was by no means as close as that. 'But his wife's gone away,' he said. 'Whatever you'd done, she isn't here to poison you or anything.'

'Ah yes,' said Josie, not wanting to be argued out of it. She seemed pleased by the thought that she might be in direct line to a ghost. 'But she might come back, mightn't she!'

Martyn threw down his shovel and started raking together the clods of weed that he had unearthed.

'I doubt it,' he said, feeling that it was he rather than Josie who would be threatened by Elaine's return. 'I doubt if she'll come back. Judging by the way George talks, she's gone for good.'

CHAPTER SIXTEEN

Another week and the clearance of the garden was almost complete. Paths and walls had emerged as if by magic so that what had been an overgrown tangle now revealed itself as a rose garden, a kitchen garden or a rockery. Little in the way of flowers or vegetables or shrubs had survived, but at least the places where they should have been were re-established. It was as if a reservoir had been drained, revealing the ruined remains of a once thriving village on its dry bed.

Martyn, too, had changed in appearance. He had been bronzed by the sun under which he had toiled for long hours, breaking off only for meals or a quick bout of sex with Josie. His brown hair had been streaked blond and his arms and hands scratched by the brambles and briars with which he had tussled. He felt fitter than he had ever been in his life and almost sad to see the end of his labours in sight.

Only one thing worried him and that was his relationship with Josie. She clearly worshipped him, complaining if they had to spend even a couple of hours apart. His arrival had changed everything for her: the White House, instead of being a bleak prison had become an idyll of sun, comfort and romance. He dreaded the thought of having to tell her that he was leaving but suspected that the sooner he did so the better. There was no prospect of a long-term relationship. He liked Josie a lot. She was a cute little lady with plenty of life about her and a figure to match. But in all kinds of ways they were opposites. He was thoughtful, passive, interested in ethics and metaphysics; she had never thought further than where her next meal, or her next screw, was coming from.

'We don't have to stay here all the time you know,' she announced suddenly one afternoon. She was lying naked on the grass, watching him as he trimmed a beech hedge. (The midges were being held at bay by an insect-repellent spray bought in town.)

'Pardon?' said Martyn, startled to find that what she was saying was so close to his own plans.

'I mean we get weekends off, don't we? I mean everybody does.'

'I suppose so.' It was not something that he had worried about.

'So we could go somewhere. For a weekend.'

Martyn pretended to consider it seriously. 'Where?' he said.

'Blackpool,' she said immediately.

He promised to give it further thought.

'What time is it?' she asked.

'Five past five,' he told her.

She swore mildly. The house might happily be left all day to gather dust but George would be back from the mortuary at half-past wanting to eat. She slid her feet into a pair of flip-flops and, picking up her can of spray, strode off towards the house.

The idea of the two of them taking a weekend trip seemed dangerous, giving weight to the impression that their relationship might become permanent. And what would George think? Though what he thought now Martyn had no idea. They had been discreet in their love-making – not difficult since they had the house to themselves for most of the time – but Martyn still suspected that their affair must be noticeable to anyone who cared to look. Or perhaps George did not care anyway?

Unfortunately, as that evening was to prove, whatever opinions George might have on that subject, there were other subjects on which he was very touchy indeed.

Josie served up a palatable version of chicken and chips and George insisted on opening a bottle of wine. He was, he said, very pleased with Martyn's work on the garden. If he should now decide to sell the house, it would be a much more attractive proposition than it had been two weeks ago.

When that bottle was finished they opened another one. Then, when that was also empty, they went into the lounge where the spirits were lined up on the sideboard.

'Josie,' said George, 'what would you like?'

'A large Bacardi and a small Coke,' she giggled.

Martyn accepted a small whisky, aware that they were all becoming drunk. Or at least he was; he had never had a good head for alcohol and felt dulled and tired. Josie, he felt sure, was pissed out of her skull.

She confirmed this by saying suddenly, 'George, I don't know whether we're going to let you sell this house, George.'

Although she always referred to him as George when speaking to Martyn, he could not remember her ever before addressing him directly as such. Certainly George himself seemed alerted by it. He put down the whisky bottle from which he had been pouring and turned to face her.

'Oh really,' he said with a polite smile. If there were one person in the room still in reasonable control of his faculties then he was that person.

'Yes, George,' said Josie. 'We might just want to live here forever, see, me and Martyn.'

She needed to be stopped. Martyn did not know what on earth she might say next and, more alarmingly, he suspected that she did not either.

'Then you two could buy the house,' said George with a tight smile.

Josie laughed. 'Get lost! We know when we're onto a good thing, don't we, Martyn?'

Martyn started to protest weakly. 'Er, come on, I don't think. . . .' But his mind was fuddled and he found it difficult to discover what it was that he wanted to say.

'Besides,' Josie was wagging a teasing finger at George who stood unsmiling before it, 'we know things, George. We know things.'

'Now hang on. . . .' Martyn tried again.

'We can stop you ever selling this house, George,' said Josie with an elaborate gesture that sent half her Bacardi and Coke flying onto the carpet. 'We can stop you doing anything we want.'

George had gone white and was standing immobile but for the

movement of his head as he looked from one to the other of them.

'So there,' said Josie. 'Cheers.' And poured the rest of her glassful down her chin and the front of her blouse.

'I see,' said George.

'Good,' said Josie.

'And what do you intend to do about it?' His words were so quiet as to be almost inaudible.

'What?' said Josie.

Martyn at last managed a word. 'Nothing,' he said. 'Nothing.'

Then, feeling George's eyes on him, he had a premonition of danger that cut through even his drunken state.

'I'll say good night,' said George quietly and, before either of them could move or say anything more, he had left the room.

'I've lost my drink,' said Josie stupidly.

'You shouldn't have said that,' said Martyn. He had been jolted by the anger and fear that Josie's words had touched off in George and found that he could think again.

'Said what?'

'Said what you said. He didn't like it.'

Josie, with a drunkard's ability to switch emotions at the drop of a hat, looked about to cry. 'I didn't mean anything, Martyn. I only meant that we knew about the ghost.'

'I know.'

'What will he do?'

'I don't know. Just have to wait and see, won't we.'

In the event there was not much to see – not immediately anyway. Josie did not appear for breakfast so that the two men were left to fend for themselves. Martyn, nursing a hang-over, wanted only black coffee; George made himself a boiled egg. What little was said was polite and unremarkable and George left for work.

Martyn went outside and sat for a while, letting the fresh air revive him. After ten minutes the side-door to the house opened and Josie came slowly out, still in her dressing-gown and with bare feet.

'God,' she said. 'My head.'

She sat beside him on the stone seat and they looked out over Arncaster.

132

'George seemed . . . well, all right,' he said.

'Why shouldn't he be?' she said, puzzled.

Martyn reminded her of what she had said the night before. But she was not one for regrets and saw no reason why anyone should hold against her sober something she had said when drunk.

The real surprise came when George returned home at five-thirty. He had driven off that morning in his white Volvo but now came back driving a sports car of about half the size. It was a Triumph TR7, just a year old, green, with a sun-roof and sporty wheels.

'Oh, didn't I tell you?' he said as they stood gaping in surprise. 'I decided to do a swop.'

Josie drifted away while Martyn, feeling that a show of interest was called for, inspected the controls and asked about the performance.

'You must have a go,' urged George, who seemed to be harbouring no ill-feelings at all from the night before. 'Take it out whenever you like. It's insured for any driver.'

Martyn thanked him and promised that he would.

The second surprise came when they were all sitting down to the evening meal, this time without wine.

'By the way,' said George, reaching for the bread, 'I'm going to have a party.'

'A party . . . ?' said Josie, taken aback.

'Yes,' he said with a smile. 'We used to have them regularly. I don't see why we shouldn't have another one.'

There was a silence.

'When were you thinking . . . ?' asked Martyn.

'Sunday. This Sunday coming.'

'But what's it for?' asked Josie, still puzzled.

'We don't need an excuse, do we?'

'No,' said Martyn.

But George continued anyway. 'And, if we do, it's my birthday on Sunday. Can always say it's that, can't we? A party for my birthday.'

133

CHAPTER SEVENTEEN

Once Josie had an idea she did not let go of it easily. Martyn might have turned aside her suggestion that they should have a weekend together in Blackpool, but that had been the beginning rather than the end of her campaign. She brought it up again the following day.

'It wouldn't cost us much. I mean we could stay anywhere. Or sleep under the pier if you like. . . .'

At last, nagged into submission, he said yes, OK, it seemed a good idea, why not.

He knew, anyway, that he would sooner or later have to tell her of his plans to leave the White House. Blackpool sounded as good a place as any to break the painful news.

'How about this weekend then?' she said immediately. And Martyn, failing to find an objection, said yes to that too.

They told George of their plans – or rather asked him for the time off that they would need – the same evening that Martyn had agreed to go. It was two days after George's surprise announcement that he intended to have a birthday party. And, to Martyn's surprise, the thought that their trip might interfere with that party seemed to be his only worry.

'It's just that I'd like you both to be here,' he said. 'I don't just mean to help out. But also as guests.'

Martyn was stuck for a moment, touched by George's wish to include them but not wanting to postpone the weekend with Josie since that would also mean postponing his planned departure.

'I don't mind,' Josie shrugged, looking to Martyn to propose a solution.

But it was George who had the answer.

'Why not take Friday and Saturday instead?' he suggested. 'Then you'll be back here for the Sunday – and for the party.'

'Well, if you don't mind. . . .' said Martyn.

'Great,' said Josie.

And it was agreed.

'And take the car,' George added. 'The new one I mean. I can get by with the Mini.'

'Oh no!' Martyn protested. 'For one thing, the Mini has a flat tyre.'

'Soon fix that,' said George. 'No, I insist you take the Triumph.'

In fact, so far from raising any objections to their trip, George seemed only concerned that it should be a success. He must have observed their liaison already and accepted it as established fact. And why not? He was, after all, their employer and not their guardian; though Martyn still felt a twinge of unease that they had somehow betrayed his trust in sleeping together under his roof.

Friday morning came and George prepared to leave for work in the green Mini, which now boasted four good tyres.

'So you'll be back tomorrow night then?' he said as he left them breakfasting in the kitchen.

'Yes,' said Martyn. 'Only are you sure about the car?'

'Positive,' said George, and went out before there could be any further argument.

'He doesn't seem to mind at all,' said Martyn to Josie.

'Why should he?' she said, amused by his difficulty in accepting the situation. 'I was never going to fancy him, was I? I mean it's no skin off his nose!'

Two hours later they were on their way, accelerating down the hill. Martyn enjoyed the novelty of the sports car, the way that he was able to push it through the tight bends. They cut across the eastern side of the town and found the motorway that would take them to Blackpool in less than an hour.

They would stay, he supposed, in a boarding-house of some kind. He was, anyway, accustomed to embarking on journeys without knowing where he would lay his head at the end of them. Josie was elated, excited out of all proportion to the brevity of their little holiday. She confided in him her childhood memories of holidays in Blackpool, before her father left them and the family broke up. It had been a time of small, innocent treats: donkey rides, the Golden Mile and, on the last morning of their holiday, a trip to the top of the Tower. He was pleased at her pleasure and began to share something of her excitement in the occasion so that he joined quite naturally in the cheer that she raised when they caught their first, distant view of Blackpool Tower.

The summer season was not yet underway but the hot spell of the past two weeks had brought a rush of early visitors so that it took them a little time to find a parking-space. The promenade was covered by a thin film of sand, over which couples strolled and past which trams came rattling. The tide was out so that the first thing they did was to go down onto the beach. They made their way between families encamped around sand-castles or attempting hopeless games of cricket.

'Never changes does it,' sighed Josie, stepping back as a wavelet came licking at her toes.

Martyn breathed deeply, savouring the ozone. 'I should think that that's half the attraction.'

They went back up to the promenade and strolled along, feeling themselves too old for the beach, but too young to sit all day in a deck-chair. Josie bought a cowboy hat and put it on.

'Don't you want one?' she urged.

'No,' said Martyn firmly. He had consented only to come with her, not to go the whole hog and wear silly hats.

He had decided to introduce her to the idea that he would soon be leaving at the beginning rather than at the end of their short holiday – that way they would have time to talk about it and come to terms with it. Leaving it till the last minute would give her the unpleasant impression that he had been deliberately keeping it from her even while they were sharing their boarding-house bed.

They ate fish and chips, lost fifty pence in a slot-machine arcade and looked out to sea through a telescope. By late afternoon, with the sun still hot on their faces, they found themselves on the Central Pier, perched on its wrought-iron seats and leaning over the rail to watch the sea crawling back in between its giant stanchions. It seemed as good a time as any.

136

'I've enjoyed doing that garden,' said Martyn, seeking a casual way in.

'Yeah?'

'Be sorry to leave it really.'

It took a moment for the inference to percolate through.

'Leave it?' said Josie, looking round at him.

'Well, can't stay forever, can I?'

'Don't see why not,' she muttered, already on the defensive.

He took a deep breath. 'I was thinking of going next week.'

'Going where?'

'Oh, I don't know. Probably back to London. Continue the absurd quest for a career before I'm too old to be considered for anything.'

'Going without me?'

Another deep breath. 'Yes,' he said quietly.

'Leaving me in that sodding house?' Her voice rose, bitter, complaining.

He managed a little laugh, hoping to keep things light. 'Not as bad as all that, is it?'

But she was beyond being joked out of her mood and only swore loudly at him, turning a few disapproving heads in their direction.

'Oh, come on, Josie. . . .' He tried to calm her.

'Bloody typical!' She was almost shouting. 'Had what you want off me and so now you're off, that's it, is it?'

He could have protested that all the first moves had been hers but doubted that that kind of academic point would carry much weight. Besides, her outburst had attracted more attention. Two ladies in nearby deck-chairs were tutting at them, while others were showing interest, hoping for a full-scale row.

'Please,' he said, 'let's just talk about it.'

But she was storming off along the pier, away from him. He could not see her face and wondered whether she was in tears. He hurried after her.

'Josie, please. . . .'

'Oh, get lost!'

She broke into a small run, her high heels clip-clopping on the wooden boards. He jogged along beside her.

137

'Look, it doesn't mean I never want to see you again! Let's go somewhere and talk about it!'

'You don't think I'm staying!' she spat at him. 'You don't think I'm stopping here now!'

Nothing he could say had any effect. They hurried together back along the promenade, she resolute and on the brink of tears, he apologetic and pleading. Holidaymakers turned and stared as they passed. She stopped only when she reached the car.

'Let me in,' she said, pulling at the locked door.

'Oh, come on,' he groaned. 'Don't let's spoil everything!'

But she was adamant and insisted: 'Let me in! Or I'll go and catch a train. You don't think I'm stopping here with you now!'

So that he had no option but to open up the car and get in alongside her. He made a last effort to salvage the situation.

'Josie, please. Look, I'm sorry I said it like that. I didn't realize that it'd be such a shock. Now, please, let's just discuss things.'

'Sod off.'

He gave up, turned the ignition key and obediently pointed the car back towards Arncaster.

They drove back in a sullen silence. Martyn felt annoyed, frustrated by the way that things had turned out. Nor was his annoyance just with Josie and her display of wilfulness. It was rather with himself and his own display of blinkered selfishness. His failure to foresee Josie's reaction was only the latest example. He had started by making love to another man's wife, lying (by omission) to that man, then making love to that same man's housekeeper under his own roof and now crowning it all by ruining Josie's treat. He could not help feeling that he had become some kind of emotional lout, wandering the country, carelessly offending and upsetting and taking advantage.

'It won't do,' he said aloud, coming to the end of his catalogue of self-condemnation.

Josie turned sharply.

'Sorry,' he said, seeing her expression. 'Talking to myself.'

These were the only words spoken between them during the whole journey. He drove fast, wanting to get it over with, and pulled up in front of the house no more than forty-five minutes after leaving Blackpool.

Josie got out without a word and went inside. He sat watching her go, then climbed out himself, relieved to be able to straighten up again after the cramped interior of the sports car. It was still a pleasant afternoon; the garden was still in its unfamiliar splendour. How could everything else have turned so sour? Martyn sighed at his own foolishness (and a little bit at Josie's too) and opened the boot to take out the small hold-all that had been their joint overnight bag.

Josie had disappeared – probably to her room; he thought it best not to investigate. Nor, fortunately, was there any sign of George; there was no knowing how Josie might have reacted to him in her black mood.

He took the hold-all up to his room and poked around inside it for the few things – electric razor, toothbrush, clean tee-shirt – that were his; Josie's he would leave for her to collect later.

It was then that he heard the faintest of sounds from above. He stopped and listened, holding his breath. The isolation of the house had accustomed him to near-perfect silence; even its mutterings of old age had been stilled in the hot weather. The sound from above had suggested a footstep; as if someone were walking about on the second floor. This would be unusual in itself: the second floor, the old servants' quarters, was virtually unused. Martyn had only been up there on that first day when Josie had shown him round the house. He had almost persuaded himself that he had been imagining things when he heard another sound. This time it was the distinctive creak of a floorboard.

His first thought was that it must be George. His second was that it could be burglars, or at least someone who had found a way in during their absence. Had they left a door unlocked? He had not noticed whether Josie, who had been first into the house, had walked straight in or had had to use her key to open the door.

Whoever it was, he felt it his duty to investigate. Stepping noiselessly in his training-shoes, he went to the end of the corridor and up the uncarpeted second flight of stairs.

From the top of those stairs he would, he knew, be able to see right the way along the top of the house. He raised his head cautiously above floor level. And saw no-one. The corridor at least was deserted.

He waited, straining to hear, then went up the remaining stairs and called tentatively: 'Hello? Anybody there?'

Again he thought he heard a movement but could not be sure. Suppose it were a cat? Or a bird that had found its way in but could not get back out? He tried again: 'Hello?'

This time there was no mistaking the sound of a door opening. Someone was coming out of one of the bedrooms at the far end of the corridor. He steeled himself, ready for anything. Anything but for what he saw.

Elaine Webster, wearing much the same outfit as when he had last seen her, came out of the room, saw him and stopped. She was carrying something in her hand.

Martyn, too amazed to speak, stared at her in open-mouthed astonishment. Had she then returned to her husband? What would she make of his presence in the house? Should he even pretend not to know her? His mind was flooded with questions, too many for him to begin to sort out before he was distracted by something else.

'What's up?'

It was Josie, coming up the stairs and nearly by his feet. She must have heard his exploratory calls and now stared on seeing the look of amazement on his face.

'What's up?' she said again, becoming frightened. 'Is there somebody there?'

Martyn did not answer. He looked back along the corridor. And saw that Elaine had gone.

Josie ran up the remaining steps and grabbed his arm. 'Who is it?'

Still Martyn could not sort out what to do or say for the best. 'I thought . . .' he stammered, 'a woman. . . .'

Josie gave a scream that made him jump. 'The ghost?' she gasped.

'No. . . .' he started to object.

But she would not be persuaded and clung to him for protection. 'Where is she then?'

'She, er. . . .' Martyn could only make a helpless gesture

140

towards the now empty corridor.

'It was the ghost!' wailed Josie. 'It must have been!'

'Oh, don't be ridiculous!' snapped Martyn, made irritable by the succession of shocks.

'Well, who else could it have been?'

This cornered him into telling a white lie.

'Well, I mean I *thought* there was somebody. Perhaps I was wrong, that's all. I thought I heard footsteps. It must have been this old house.'

'No, Martyn. No, it must have been the ghost!' jabbered Josie. 'Come on down! Come on, let's get out!'

He sighed at the stupidity of the idea. He felt sure that the woman he had seen had been flesh and blood. All the more so since it was flesh that he had once touched and enjoyed. He could not, however, explain that to Josie. Nor did he know what hares might be started by his even admitting that the woman he had seen was Elaine Webster, George's wife. Perhaps she was returning in secret and would not want her presence announced, least of all by the young male hitch-hiker she had seduced and then never expected to set eyes on again.

'Just wait there,' he said to Josie.

But she gave another wail of dismay and kept her tight grip on his arm, going with him as he went down the corridor, peering into the rooms. Some were totally empty with neither carpets nor curtains; others were full of junk; all were dusty and faintly damp-smelling. But Elaine Webster was in none of them. She had vanished as quickly as she had come.

CHAPTER EIGHTEEN

'Well, I don't know whether she was a ghost or not,' said Rob. 'But one thing I do know.'

'What?' asked Martyn.

'It's your round.'

Martyn laughed, collected their empty glasses and went to the bar. They were in the Boot and Shoe; it was Saturday lunchtime and the public bar was full of men with racing papers.

There had been no further sightings of Elaine the previous night. Whether ghost or real live woman, she had disappeared without trace. Martyn had finally managed to calm Josie – with the help of an illicit Bacardi and Coke – and when George arrived home at nine o'clock that night they told him nothing of what had happened. Martyn, still with no clue as to what Elaine might have been doing there, did not want to be the one to announce her arrival to a husband who had seemed quite content that she should stay away forever. And he managed to convince Josie that no householder liked to be told of a ghost on the premises.

A side-effect, for which he was grateful, had been the ending of hostilities between them. In fact, too frightened to sleep by herself, Josie had crept to his room and joined him in his bed for the whole of that night.

Rob had been intrigued by Martyn's account of the ghost-like visitation, while Martyn was glad of the chance to obtain an objective view on things. He filled Rob in on the background, telling him about the reputation for female ghosts that the house already enjoyed. Rob was agnostic as far as ghosts went and was happy to debate the pros and cons of this particular one till closing time. By the time Martyn returned from the crowded bar with their drinks he had been able to think further.

'It's a question of choosing the simplest explanation to fit the facts,' he said, then took a drink of the offered pint. 'Cheers.'

'Occam's Razor,' said Martyn in agreement. Then added in response to Rob's blank look, 'It's a principle of logic. More or less what you said.'

'Good,' said Rob.

'So we only seriously consider the ghost theory after we've eliminated every other possibility.' This kind of logical approach was right up his street. 'So long as it's possible that it actually *was* his wife that I saw, then we have to assume that that was in fact the case.'

'Anything's possible though, isn't it,' said Rob vaguely.

'Anything's *logically* possible,' Martyn corrected him. 'Doesn't mean it is in practice.'

Rob had a drink and thought about it. 'If, for example, she'd been dead,' he said, 'it couldn't have been her if she'd been dead at the time.'

Martyn gave way on that point but reminded him that they had no reason for believing Elaine Webster to be dead, that the drowned body that had so interested the police had proved not to be her, and that he, Martyn, had seen her and talked to her as lately as May fifth. They had every reason, therefore, for assuming that she was alive, and that she would have been perfectly capable of having visited the White House the previous evening.

'It would,' he conceded, 'be a different story if she were dead.'

Rob grunted in agreement and began to roll himself a cigarette. 'So how had she got in?' he asked.

Martyn shrugged. There was surely little problem there. 'Presumably she still has her own key.'

'And how did she get out? I mean without you seeing her?'

'Well, there are two flights of stairs in the house, one at each end. We'd come up one, so I suppose that she must have slipped away down the other.'

'OK, so what was she doing there? Why come and go like that?'

'No idea,' said Martyn, though, of course, he had. Looked at

143

from Elaine's point of view, his presence there must have been a terrible shock: she returns to the family home to discover that her partner in a casual affair that had taken place at the other end of the country was in residence . . . ! Little wonder that she fled. Though this still left the question of what she had come back for in the first place.

'Perhaps,' said Rob, staring into his pint, 'it was a sign.'

'Of what?'

'That she *is* dead.'

'How do you work that out?'

'I don't. I'm just saying. If she was a ghost then that might have been why she'd appeared. To tell you that she was dead. Of course she didn't know that the first person who'd see her would be a logical bugger like you who refused to believe in ghosts altogether!'

Martyn laughed. 'Must be frustrating to be a ghost when no-one believes in you!'

And they let the matter drop, having said all that there was to be said on the subject. Rob wanted to get another round in but Martyn insisted that he was going. Lunchtime drinking made him sleepy and left him with a headache. He had ended up in the pub only because there had been no-one in at Rob and Samantha's home when he had gone there to invite them to George's party. Samantha, it turned out, was out shopping; Rob was reading *The Guardian* in the Boot and Shoe and was glad to see Martyn.

'Don't forget then. Any time after eight tomorrow night,' said Martyn, now leaving.

'Yeah. Cheers. Though I must say I haven't heard of many blokes who give birthday parties. I think my last one was when I was seven!'

Martyn felt obliged to explain on George's behalf. 'Oh, I think that's only an excuse. Apparently they were always giving parties before his wife went. I think he just wants to show that he's got over her leaving him.'

'Be funny if she turns up, won't it,' said Rob.

Martyn hesitated. It was a thought that had already occurred to him but it had seemed less amusing than uncomfortably embarrassing.

'I don't suppose for a minute that she will,' he said.

'Sam'll be pleased,' said Rob. 'We don't get invited to many parties nowadays.'

Martyn left him and set out back to the White House.

George had been keen that he and Josie should invite friends of their own. Josie had said that there was no-one she wanted to invite so that Martyn had felt obliged to supply someone. And anyway it pleased him that he should see Rob and Samantha again before he left the town for pastures new. He worried lest Rob still suspected that there had been something between him and Samantha. Meeting both of them in the public setting of a party might lay at least that ghost to rest.

And it looked as though it was going to be a party to be remembered. George had been ferrying in supplies all day so that Martyn got back to find the kitchen piled high with food and drink. Mrs Bolton had been called in to help Josie get the place spick and span, and George had unearthed some ageing garden furniture.

'Be nice not to have to apologize for the state of the garden,' he said as Martyn went to help him carry it.

'How many will there be coming?' asked Martyn.

'Oh, fifty or sixty. Some people have said they're not sure if they can make it.'

It was later that afternoon, almost too late with the shops closing at five-thirty, that Martyn had a thought.

'We should buy him present,' he said to Josie.

'Who?'

'George. It's his birthday tomorrow. We should buy him a birthday present.'

'He's too old for presents,' she objected.

But Martyn persisted: if *they* did not buy him anything then who else would? It was the least they could do after the employment and the hospitality that he had given them.

Josie was reluctantly converted and they hurried into town, taking the Triumph. They wandered round the town, joining the last, hectic rush of Saturday shoppers. It was not easy to decide on something suitable. They ended up in a book shop but the murder mysteries that Josie selected struck Martyn as being in possible bad taste.

'I mean with him being a mortician. He might think we're making a joke about his job.'

'Well, how about this then?' said Josie and held up a book of ghost stories.

Martyn gave a little laugh, glad that she could bring herself to joke about the subject. 'We've got enough of our own ghost stories,' he said.

'We've got ghosts to write 'em as well,' countered Josie.

He looked at her anxiously and was relieved to see that she was grinning.

Eventually, with time pressing, they settled on a box of cigarettes and some handkerchiefs, hardly original but certainly acceptable and that seemed the next best thing. They also bought a card with a seascape on the front and wrote, 'To George. Happy Birthday and Best Wishes from Josie and Martyn,' inside it. Back at the house, Josie took their purchases and hid them in her bedroom.

The weather forecast said that after some overnight rain it would again be warm and dry. The kitchen was full of food waiting to be set out and bottles waiting to be opened. All seemed on course for a successful party. Martyn for one hoped that it would be and that Elaine would not reappear – whether in human or in spiritual form – to upset the apple-cart. George Webster had had a difficult time of late. He surely deserved that his birthday party at least should go off without a hitch.

CHAPTER NINETEEN

They gave him his card and present at breakfast the following morning. Or rather Martyn did. Josie had insisted that it had been his idea and that she would not know what to say.

'Happy birthday,' had been all that Martyn could think of.

'Thank you,' said George, surprised.

He turned the parcel over in his hands, either suspicious of it or not knowing how to get the string off. Then he took the plunge and, tearing at the paper, found his way to the handkerchiefs and cigarettes.

'You're not easy to choose something for,' said Martyn with an apologetic laugh.

'I don't suppose I am,' said George, who seemed even more embarrassed by the small ceremony than they were.

He read the card, then, without a word, stood it on the nearest kitchen-shelf to hand, next to a jar of spaghetti.

Mrs Bolton arrived and the preparations for the party were resumed. Martyn read the Sunday papers, looking particularly in the Situations Vacant columns but finding nothing that seemed even a remote possibility. Josie had been press-ganged into working in the kitchen so that they saw little of one another. She seemed, anyway, to have forgiven him for his unwitting sabotage of their Blackpool trip. Or perhaps she had simply forgotten all about it. Martyn wondered if he should go suddenly and without fuss the following morning but was unable to decide. The party, the time for which was now approaching rapidly, seemed to have imposed itself between present and future. He would have to wait till it was over before attempting to plan anything.

By early evening all was ready and waiting. Mrs Bolton had gone home, they had retired to their separate rooms and the house was quiet. Even Josie, who had earlier affected indifference to the party; had relented and gone to put on what she derisively called her 'best frock'.

Martyn shaved, put on a clean tee-shirt and the least worn of his two pairs of jeans. Then, still faintly uneasy at the possibility of Elaine staging a reappearance, he took the opportunity to slip quiety upstairs to the top floor. He went cautiously along the corridor, peering into each room in turn; but there was no-one there. Nor were there any ghosts. He came to the end, went down the back stairs and returned to his room.

Pulling on his wrist watch, he noticed that it was exactly seven-thirty. Again he wished fervently that the party would go well. Mixed with which was a wish that it should be over. For a moment he found himself repeating one of the little tricks of his childhood: visiting the dentist, he would look at the town-hall clock and wish with all his might that it should move magically forward to the time that he would be coming out again. It was now his wrist watch that he willed to jump from early evening to early morning.

'Ha!' He gave a little laugh at his childish urge, wondering why the approaching party should weigh so heavily upon him. All parties were nervous affairs certainly, and he did not want George to be hurt by the failure of this one. But there was no need to get into such a sweat about it.

Thinking that the fresh air might help, he went out onto the front lawn. Church bells were just audible from the town. It was a peaceful evening of early summer. Martyn looked out over the now familiar view, knew that he had outstayed his welcome and wondered whether, once he had left tomorrow or the day after, he would ever return.

To his surprise, George appeared on the lawn beside him. He had put on a cravat for his role of host and, Martyn thought, seemed nervous about the night ahead.

'I was thinking about Elaine,' said George unexpectedly. 'My wife.'

'Yes?' said Martyn, taken by surprise.

'Have you told anyone else about her?'

'About seeing her?'

'Yes?'

Martyn hesitated, not sure what George was getting at, wondering if this could even be a reference to the Friday night and Elaine's manifestation on the top floor.

'The police, for example?' said George. He, too, was looking outwards over the town so that their eyes did not meet.

'Oh no,' said Martyn. 'No, I didn't, no.'

There was a long silence as if a further question was hanging between them, though what it could be Martyn had no idea and therefore could not answer it. For want of something to say he was on the point of mentioning that he would soon be leaving but, even as he was framing this announcement in his mind, there was the sound of a car and the first of the guests was arriving, releasing them both from the awkward situation.

In fact it was Kevin, the young man whom Martyn had previously seen in the mortuary. His ageing Volkswagen rumbled in complaint against the long climb up the hill.

'Come in,' called George. 'You're the first!'

But already another car had pulled through the gates. Martyn relaxed slightly, feeling that the party was, after all, going to be a success. He went inside and put on a record of songs from *Cabaret*. Josie came into the lounge as he was doing so.

'Well?' she asked.

He looked round and saw that she had coloured green a swathe of hair going from over her left eyebrow to her right ear.

'Great,' he said.

'You're sure?' she asked, clearly relieved.

'Yes,' he said. And meant it; there was something about Josie that suited a splash of livid colour.

'Well, I can always wash it out,' she said, pleased. 'But I thought I'd try it. And I mean it is a party when all's said and done.'

There were other cars arriving outside and distant shrieks of greeting. Martyn and Josie stayed where they were, in tacit agreement that the party should find them rather than they it.

A middle-aged couple came to the door of the lounge, saw them and moved away again.

'All right, be like that,' called Josie, now out to enjoy herself.

The house was filling with people, all of whom seemed to know one another though one or two seemed uncertain about George, who hung around outside, supervising the parking, greeting his guests and directing them in towards the alcohol. No-one, of course, knew Martyn or Josie, until Rob and Samantha drifted in carrying a wrapped bottle of wine and looking for somewhere to put it down.

'Oh great,' said Martyn in greeting and introduced them to Josie.

'Pleased to meet you,' said Rob, who seemed taken aback, though whether by the green hair or what Martyn could not be sure.

Samantha nodded, gave an icy little smile and said, 'Well, this is a night of surprises.'

'Let's get you something to drink then,' said Martyn, ushering them into the kitchen.

'Thought you'd never ask,' said Rob.

There was already a *mêlée* round the drinks table and Martyn found himself standing next to a tall man – an inch or so taller than himself in fact – who suddenly turned and introduced himself as Lawrence Cut or Cup, Martyn could not be sure.

'You a friend of old George's then?' he asked Martyn.

'I've been staying here. Working on the garden,' said Martyn simply. But Lawrence had turned away, distracted by the arrival of someone else.

'It's that bloody gang of thespians,' said Samantha when Martyn got back to them with the drinks.

'Pardon?'

'Harlequins or something they call themselves. I recognise one or two of them.'

'I wonder who all the others are,' said Martyn, gazing round. Some of them, he guessed, must be from the hospital. Others, one or two with a subversive air about them as if they should not have been there at all, were probably friends of Elaine's who had come to see how George had survived her departure. 'Very brave of him. . . .' was a phrase that Martyn heard as he moved past a conspiring group.

'I know him,' said Samantha slowly. Then, as it came to her, she exclaimed, 'Charlesworth!'

'Charles who?' asked Rob.

'Worth. He's the pathologist – one of them anyway – for this area. Charlesworth.'

They all looked at the man she indicated, who was wearing a suit and standing alone across the room.

'George's boss then,' said Martyn.

'What's a pathologist?' asked Josie.

'Why don't you ask him?' said Samantha before Martyn could begin to explain.

'OK,' said Josie, taking up the challenge. 'I will.' And she marched across to him.

They saw his startled reaction but were then pleased (in Martyn's case) and disappointed (in Samantha's) to see him settle down to talk animatedly to her.

'Anybody else ready for another?' enquired Rob on his way back into the kitchen.

Samantha gave him a black look, Martyn shook his head and he had gone, leaving them together, though mercifully not alone: the room held at least another twenty people, including Josie and Mr Charlesworth who were now laughing together at something.

'So that's Josie then, is it,' said Samantha.

'Yes,' said Martyn evenly. 'She's a sort of housekeeper here.'

'I'll bet she is. I wouldn't have said she was your style but then there's no accounting for taste is there?'

To which Martyn merely smiled, then excused himself – 'I seem to be in charge of the records' – and moved away. He felt that he owed Josie at least that little show of loyalty.

In fact the party had already reached a pitch where background music no longer mattered. Everyone who had been invited seemed to have come, and perhaps some others besides, for even the White House seemed full to bursting. The party had expanded outwards from the kitchen, its food-and-drink-laden heart, spread through all the downstairs rooms and flowed out through the french windows and into the garden. A soft dusk had replaced the bright daylight, warm and calm.

'Oh look, isn't this lovely!' called out a tall girl in a white dress on discovering the old rose garden with its chipped stone figures.

Suddenly the size of the place had given the evening a feel, not of a private party, but of a public assembly; a carnival even. People were letting themselves go. By nine o'clock it was a noisy, rollocking affair on a grand scale.

'We seem to be running out of mixers,' said George, coming to find Martyn where he was sitting with Josie on the wall outside. They had found one another again, lost Rob, Samantha and Mr Charlesworth and come to sit away from most of the frolicking. The course of the party had surprised and slightly stunned them both: the stolid middle-aged gathering that they had expected had transmogrified into a high-spirited riot.

'Running out of what?' asked Josie.

'Mixers.'

'You mean fruit juices, things like that?' asked Martyn.

George nodded. 'Can you look after things while I dash over to that off-licence in Ballantyne Street? They keep pub hours. I should catch them before they close.'

'But we had tons of fruit juice!' objected Josie.

'Not any more,' said George.

'Look, I'll go,' offered Martyn. And, as George began to protest, 'I'd much rather do that than stay here in charge of this lot!'

'Oh well. . . .' George hesitated, then gave way. 'Thanks very much. Perhaps Josie'll go and keep you company.'

Josie said she would: 'Don't know anybody else here, do I!'

George gave Martyn some money and the two of them hurried to the Triumph. The Mini was hemmed in by a dozen other cars even had they wished to take it. The Triumph, parked right up to the gateway, had a clear way out.

'Should have time,' said Martyn, looking at his watch. It was a relief to slam the car doors and feel that they were getting away for a while from the noisy throng.

Martyn put the key in the ignition, then hesitated.

'I shouldn't be driving, you know.'

'Why not?' asked Josie, looking at him in surprise.

'I must have had more than two pints. I mean the equivalent of.'

'What, you!' she said in amused scorn. 'Even I drink more than you do!'

'I know but. . . .'

'And then you've been eating as well!'

He accepted her arguments and turned the key. 'I'll take it easy anyway,' he said, as they moved forward through the gate and began the steep descent. The wing mirror gave him a quick glimpse of George standing watching them go, a hand raised in salute.

'Don't you need your lights on?' asked Josie with a grin.

'Oh yes,' he said, surprised at having to be reminded. Perhaps the drink had affected him, even if he were legally below the limit. He would have to be careful.

Josie gave a laugh, pleased to have caught him out. She rested an affectionate hand on his thigh.

The headlights showed the road falling away before them, straight for most of the way, then twisting to accommodate ancient boundaries before it would eventually join the more orderly street pattern of the town below. It was a helter-skelter that Martyn had come to know. His foot moved over to the brake-pedal without his being aware of it as they approached the first bend. He only became aware as the pedal refused to yield or the car to slow.

'Christ!' he gasped as he pulled them through the bend, the tyres emitting a thin shriek of protest.

'What?' said Josie, unperturbed.

'No brakes . . . !' gasped Martyn, now straining against the pedal.

'What?' She was still not afraid; did not know whether to believe him; was on her guard against a practical joke.

'It's stuck!' he shouted, and there was now no room for disbelief as he fought desperately to keep the accelerating car in contact with the road.

Josie screamed and grabbed at him, pulling him across the seat towards her.

'Get off!' he yelled, and pushed her violently away. The car, magnifying their struggle, swayed into the side and struck the low stone wall that ran along that section of the road. There was a rasping of metal and a shower of sparks before they rebounded, almost hit the opposite banking and then miraculously found the middle of the road again.

Josie was screaming steadily, her head buried in her hands. Martyn's head was lodged against the low roof of the car as he was as near to standing on the brake pedal as he could get in that confined cockpit, every ounce of his strength directed downwards through his right foot. But to no avail; the pedal gave not one jot, the speedometer swung up to over seventy while a hundred yards ahead there was the road's sharpest bend, the one that they could not possibly take.

He grabbed the gear lever but the engine howled in rage at his attempt to force it into a lower gear and threw the lever back at him with such force that he lost his grip and was pawing empty air.

There was nothing more to do but wait for death. A fragment of a prayer flashed into his mind – '. . . . Forgive us our trespasses as we forgive those that trespass against us. . . .' – then a bewilderingly compressed vision of a past life that he barely recognized as the one that he was about to lose: a seven-year-old, proud in his prep school uniform; a sixth-former with spots; a student in hired cap and gown for graduation day. All culminating in this rush to death with a girl with green hair huddled screaming in the seat beside him.

They were moving too fast for him to recognise the shape in the road until after they had hit it.

The headlights caught it – a small hill hurtling to meet them – then there was a solid thud that checked their speed and sent him bumping forward against the steering wheel. It was a steering wheel that had a life of its own, squirming away from his grip as the car, deflected by the collision, finally left the road.

A cow, Martyn told himself as the windscreen fragmented in front of him letting in a charge of air and a terrifying din that was a mixture of car engine and crashing branches. It had been a cow that they had hit.

The car thumped down under them, then lurched and rolled sickeningly. It did, however, confirm that they were not yet dead.

The realisation of a possible reprieve brought a spray of adrenalin to Martyn. He grabbed the steering wheel again with one hand and, with the other, switched off the ignition. Almost unbelievably the engine stopped. There was now just the lurching and the bumping and the rush of wind.

They were, he told himself, in a field and still alive – though still hurtling along at a dangerous lick. One of the headlights had gone, but in the other he saw a hedge looming up across their path. His instinct was to try and turn and his hands had even begun to do so before his judgement stopped him. He braced himself, flung a restraining arm across the now silent Josie and allowed the car to plough into the mass of hawthorn.

They stopped.

The feeling of relief was the sweetest thing that he had ever tasted. Together with the sudden quiet and stillness that had descended, it tempted him to stay where he was, to relax, to close his eyes and savour the life that was still within him.

Till he remembered the danger that they might both be in from petrol dripping from the wrecked engine. And Josie. What sort of state was she in? He was aware that her screaming had stopped somewhere along the way; he now saw that she was unconscious, slumped forward, and bleeding from a cut across her forehead.

One of his hands had blood on it too as he opened the door. Getting out, his legs gave beneath him, but it was only a reaction to the force that he had been exerting through them and after a moment he was able to scramble back to his feet and go round to open Josie's door. Despite its battered surface, it opened easily and he was able to lift Josie out and carry her a safe distance away from the car. Her pulse and breathing seemed strong enough. She must have struck her head on the windscreen at some point, and one of her feet seemed oddly twisted.

In leaning in to pull her out, he had glanced at the murderous brake-pedal and caught sight of what seemed to be a wedge beneath it, but one that gleamed and seemed strangely translucent. Now that he had lifted Josie clear, the priority was to get help, but he could not resist quickly returning first to the car and, after checking that there was no sight or sound of anything untoward going on under the bonnet, he leaned in again and slid a hand under the pedal.

What he felt was so unexpected – cold and wet and hard – that he jerked his hand away again. Then he realized what it was.

A block of ice had been jammed beneath the pedal making any movement of it impossible. It was already running with water, melting from the heat around it and the pressure that it had withstood.

He turned, looked to see that Josie seemed comfortable on the banking at the side of the field where he had left her, and started jogging back towards the road for help.

The ice, he realized as he ran, had been a cleverly chosen weapon. Had it not been for a cow – God rest its soul – that had chosen to sit down for a rest in the middle of the road, then he and Josie would have left the road at eighty miles an hour another fifty yards along. And the car would have flown through the air like a bird before dropping into a small quarry. It would have exploded, there would have been a fire and the ice would have melted away. There would have been no evidence of the sabotage that would have killed them. And had not Martyn, after all, just come from a rowdy party? What was more understandable than that, driving a sports car down an unlit road, he should have misjudged a bend with fatal results? The ice would have gone, leaving not the smallest tell-tale clue to be sifted from the wreckage.

It would have been the perfect double murder.

CHAPTER TWENTY

As the evening wore on, the mood of the party mellowed. The slightly desperate air of gaiety subsided and was replaced by a quieter one. Conversations became confidential, people stopped charging like dervishes around the gardens, returned inside and settled into groups and couples. Somebody put a record of smoochy music on in the lounge and those who were that way inclined went in there to dance, shuffling around on the unsuitably thick carpet. There was still plenty of drink though the food had run out. One or two people looked at their watches and wondered aloud about babysitters. It seemed that the end of the evening was beginning.

That was until Martyn arrived back in a police car.

It was a conspicuous red and white, with POLICE stencilled in letters a foot high across it. Blue lights flashed from its roof. Those at the front of the house stared curiously as it slid to a halt and then called out to others, so that there was a small, inquisitive crowd to greet Martyn as, looking somewhat torn and bruised, he stepped out, accompanied by Detective Sergeant Bradbury and Detective Constable Woods.

'What's happened?'

'Has there been an accident?'

'Is anybody hurt?'

There was an excited rush of questions to which Martyn gave only a weak smile and which the two policemen ignored. There was a moment of indecision as they looked round, then George appeared, his face white and set.

'Mr Webster,' said Bradbury, 'can we have a word?'

'What's happened?' said George.

The news of their arrival had now spread to everyone. The last to hear of it were still coming out to see what was happening, their voices raised until they were shushed by the rest who were waiting to hear Bradbury's answer.

'There's been an accident,' he said.

'Oh no,' said George.

'Nobody seriously hurt but we'd like to talk to you about it.'

'Where's Josie?' asked George.

Martyn answered. 'In hospital. But nothing serious. They think it's just a broken ankle; that and possible concussion.'

There was a murmur among the spectators as this news was conveyed to those at the back who could not hear what was being said.

Bradbury turned to his companion. 'I think it'd be best if nobody left until we get this sorted.'

'Right,' said Woods, looking round at the little crowd of revellers, some of whom had brought their drinks out with them.

Bradbury addressed them.

'Ladies and gentlemen, can I just ask you not to leave until we've found out what we need to know. I can assure you we won't keep you any longer than is necessary.'

Most nodded eagerly: to stay and be in on the mystery was exactly what they wanted. Only the odd voice murmured apologetically, and regretfully, about babysitters and having to leave.

'If any of you really must go,' went on Bradbury in response, 'then make sure that Constable Woods here knows that you're going and has your names and addresses.' He turned to George. 'Can we find somewhere private?'

The guests parted to let them through as George led the way into the house, Martyn and then Detective Sergeant Bradbury following. Constable Woods stayed where he was and folded his arms in the manner of one resigned to waiting patiently.

A hubbub of conversation arose from the guests. This was an unexpected development indeed, an unscheduled and very welcome infusion of high drama. And, since there was no-one

158

seriously hurt, there was no call for them to remain solemn about it. The house filled again with shouts and laughter as they poured back inside, heading for the kitchen to replenish their drinks.

George led the other two into the old billiards-room which, at the back of the house, was furthest from the noise. Bradbury closed the door and then remained standing while George and Martyn perched on the uncomfortable bench seats that lined the walls.

'For goodness sake,' said George, 'will somebody please tell me what's happened!'

Bradbury seemed about to speak, then changed his mind and gave a small nod to Martyn, who took it as his cue and began to relate the story of the accident. He told about the failure of the brakes, the intervention of the cow and his discovery of the lump of ice; and about his running the remaining mile or so to the town from where he had telephoned the police; who had picked him up, taken him back to the scene of the accident and summoned an ambulance for Josie.

'I don't know what sort of state the car's in,' he ended apologetically. 'Bit of a mess I would think.'

But George's mind was not on the condition of the car. He had sat listening throughout without a word and now asked, 'So somebody had wedged this lump of ice there to make sure that whoever next drove the car would be killed?'

Martyn gave a small shrug. That was certainly the way it looked to him. But what would that then mean? He had had time, while waiting for the police and ambulance to arrive, to consider some of the ramifications and found none of them easy. Was it then one of the sixty or so guests who had placed the ice there? And, if so, whose foot had they expected to be above it on the brake pedal? It was, after all, George's car, not his. Had it then been an attempt to kill George which had backfired in more ways than one?'

'Unfortunately,' said Bradbury, 'by the time we got to the scene of the accident there was only a very small piece of ice lying on the floor of the car. And, needless to say, that's gone now.'

Martyn gave a sigh of impatience. It was not the first hint he had been given that his story was only half-believed. The other, younger policeman, he was sure, considered him a dangerous driver who had nearly killed himself and his girl-friend then had simply dreamed up the ice-under-the-brake-pedal story as an ingenious excuse. Martyn had already been breathalised and, mercifully, found to be just under the limit.

'It was a block of ice,' he said patiently. 'Must have been six inches thick to start with.'

'Well, so you say,' said Bradbury.

Martyn made a little gesture of helplessness. Not that he blamed Bradbury or even resented his cynical attitude; he could appreciate the difficulty of evidence that melted away to nowhere. But it still came hard that, on top of narrowly surviving a murder attempt, he should now be accused of fabricating one.

'Mr Webster,' said Bradbury, 'do you know anything about this ice business?'

'Me?' said George in surprise. 'Well . . . no.'

'I mean it was your car.'

'Yes.'

'And we're told by Mr Culley that, in fact, you were intending to drive it. And that you would have done so except that he offered to go in your place.'

'Yes,' agreed George.

'So that, if we accept that there was a block of ice put there to kill whoever was driving it, then it might seem, might it not, that you were the intended victim and not Mr Culley?'

George nodded slowly.

'Can you think of anyone here tonight who might have done such a thing?'

This time, equally slowly, George shook his head.

Bradbury turned back to Martyn. 'On the other hand,' he said with the air of a man wanting to get all the cards clearly displayed on the table, 'if there was no ice then it's a simple traffic accident. And we can all save ourselves a lot of trouble and go home.'

This, it seemed, he would very much like to do.

'I'm sorry,' began Martyn. Then wondered why he should feel that need to apologise and began again, 'Look, there was some ice when you got there, yes? Not a lot but *some*?'

Bradbury nodded. 'Only it's just possible,' he said, 'that you could have brought that with you from the party and placed it on the floor of the car yourself after the accident had happened. I'm not saying that you did but I'm saying that it's possible.'

'Why on earth should I carry a piece of ice with me?' exclaimed Martyn.

'No idea,' said Bradbury frankly. 'But, then again, people do carry all kinds of strange things with them away from parties. Believe me.'

Martyn felt weary and unable to argue. Besides, he suspected that there was little point. The ice had gone for good, leaving only his word that it had ever been there. Even Josie had not been conscious to see it. It seemed inevitable that, unless something else turned up pretty quickly, then the well-meaning but down-to-earth Detective Sergeant would see himself as having no option but to report a simple road traffic accident and get himself off home to bed.

'If somebody wanted to make a big block of ice,' asked Bradbury of George, 'have you got somewhere that they could do it?'

'Well, yes,' said George. 'There's the big freezer out in the garage and the small one in the kitchen.'

Bradbury scratched his chin, gave a thoughtful grunt, then took out and lit a cigarette. 'Did anyone else know that you were going to drive into town?' he asked George.

George hesitated. 'Well, I suppose I did mention to a few people that I was going to have to go to the off-licence, yes.'

'Did you notice anyone slip outside after they'd heard you say that?' asked Bradbury in a voice of forlorn hope.

'No.'

Martyn gave him credit for trying but could still see nothing coming of it. He also realized that he was thirsty, not for alcohol but for anything. It had been an hour since the accident and the strain of it and the aftermath was telling.

'Could I possibly get a drink?' he asked.

Bradbury seemed surprised by the request, thought about it, then said, 'Don't see why not.'

'Anybody else want anything?' asked Martyn but no-one did. He came out of the billiards-room and became immediately the centre of attention as heads turned expectantly in his direction. There was a muttering of speculation but none of them knew him well enough to come out with it and ask what was going on. And there was precious little that he could have told them anyway.

Coming into the hallway *en route* to the kitchen, he heard voices raised, one of which was familiar to him.

It was Rob. Rob, half-drunk, and in loud argument with Constable Woods.

'There he is!' he shouted, catching sight of Martyn. 'You ask him yourself!'

Martyn hesitated, not sure whether to ignore this, then saw that the constable was coming towards him, followed by Rob, with a large, interested group of spectators in tow.

Martyn waited for them to reach him. 'I'm just going to get a drink,' he said to Woods, feeling that his little walkabout needed explanation.

'Tell him about seeing his wife!' instructed Rob loudly. He had indeed had more than his fair share of the drink. Martyn noticed Samantha behind him, wearing the long-suffering look of one who had witnessed such scenes before.

'All right, all right,' said Woods to Rob, then turned to Martyn. 'This gentleman says that you saw Mr Webster's wife here earlier this weekend.'

'Yes!' urged Rob.

'Now, is that true?' asked Woods.

'Yes,' admitted Martyn.

The possible relevance of Elaine's reappearance to his own near death was one from which his mind had shied away. That she should have sabotaged the car, that she should have secretly returned with the express purpose of killing her husband, made sense of a kind, but it was a kind that Martyn did not wish to contemplate.

'You saw her in this house?' asked Woods.

'Yes.'

'Told you!' shouted Rob.

'Have you told Sergeant Bradbury this?' asked Woods.

'No,' said Martyn, then added, 'It didn't seem relevant.'

162

'Well, I think you'd better let us be the judge of that,' remarked Woods. 'Where is Sergeant Bradbury now?'

And Martyn led him and his entourage, which by now comprised most of the guests, back to the billiards-room.

'If it wasn't her then it was her bloody ghost!' exclaimed Rob to the world at large.

'Who? Elaine Webster?' asked someone else who had come late on the scene.

A chorus assured her that, yes, George Webster's wife had returned and had been seen in the house.

The babble of speculation that followed this was one that Martyn was happy to escape from back into the billiards-room, even if it did mean foregoing his drink. This time, Constable Woods came with him.

'What's the matter?' asked Bradbury in surprise on seeing them.

'This man,' said Woods, indicating Martyn, 'says that he saw this man's wife' – indicating George – 'in this house on Friday night.'

Both of the other two men took a moment to realize the significance.

'I see,' said Bradbury thoughtfully.

The effect on George was more dramatic. He gave a little groan, turned even whiter if that were possible and looked to be on the point of fainting.

'You all right, George?' asked Martyn, going to him.

He said nothing, looked at Martyn, then buried his head in his hands.

Bradbury gave him a moment, then said with quiet insistence, 'You didn't know she was here, sir?'

George finally looked up and said softly, 'My wife?' as if still unsure of what they could be saying.

'Your wife,' said Bradbury gently. 'Have you seen her at all since you came to us to tell us that she'd left you?'

'No.'

'Have you heard from her at all?'

'No.'

'So if she was here at any time this weekend you didn't know

163

anything about it?'

'No.'

Bradbury paced across the wooden floor, then stopped to light another cigarette. 'You are sure it was her?' he said to Martyn.

Martyn nodded. He felt a sense of justification in that this new information was forcing them to reconsider seriously his claims about the existence of the lump of ice. But he knew it to be a petty and selfish reaction, one of which he was not particularly proud. What of poor George? As if it had not been bad enough that his wife had deserted him, how much worse was the possibility that she had now returned to make an attempt on his life?

In fact it was George who, without raising his eyes to look at him, asked him the next question.

'The woman that you saw in this house on Friday night. . . .'

'Yes?'

'She was the same one you gave a lift to in London?'

'Yes.'

'You are certain?' asked Bradbury again.

'Positive,' said Martyn.

George gave a heavy sigh and a shake of the head, then folded his arms in front of him and stared fixedly at the floor. It was the action of the man brought face to face with a dreadful truth.

It was left to Constable Woods, who was picking absently at the carvings on the old mantelpiece, to advance the argument.

'Whoever left that ice,' he said, 'did it tonight. It can't have been planted on Friday or else it would have melted.'

As though stung into action by this indisputable fact, Bradbury said, 'Oh well,' threw his cigarette into the empty firegrate and moved to the door. 'We'd better have a search,' he said, mainly to Woods. 'Get on to the station and get some more men here.' And he went out.

Martyn, about to follow, turned first to George to see how he was. 'You all right, George?'

George looked up at him, gave a little, sad smile and said with what was almost a laugh, 'A search . . . ! They're going to search the house for her!'

Martyn could only take this as a reference to the difficulty of such an undertaking: firstly, because of the geography of the meandering house, and, secondly, because it was still full to the brim with half-sozzled guests.

But both problems were already well on their way to being taken care of. When Martyn came out into the hall he found Detective Sergeant Bradbury protesting in vain about a search party of guests, led by Lawrence Cutt, that was about to launch itself on the very task for which Woods was supposed to be sending to the station for extra men. Apparently the discussion going on outside the billiards-room had come to the same conclusion as that inside it – that Elaine Webster might well be still on the premises, and that there was only one way to find out.

It was just the sort of challenge to appeal to a small mob of intoxicated party-goers.

'Anybody coming with me outside?' shouted Rob, who had obtained a torch from somewhere. There were a few shouts of 'Yes' in response.

'The rest of us will start right at the top of the house and work down,' Lawrence Cutt instructed his group. 'Anybody who sees her must yell out.'

'All right,' said Bradbury, seeing that he had no way of stopping them and anyway unable to search the place without help from somewhere. 'But if anybody spots her then let me know. Don't try and tackle her yourself!'

'Don't worry, Inspector,' said Lawrence, patting him on the shoulder. 'We're just the posse. You're the sheriff.'

This got a thin cheer from the assembled searchers.

'Right, this way!' shouted Lawrence, and, hand held aloft in the manner of a travel courier, he led most of the group up the stairs.

'Everybody coming outside follow me!' shouted Rob, switched on his torch and stumbled towards the door. Then hesitated. 'Does anybody know what this woman looks like?'

One or two of his followers, who included Madeleine Cummings and Maurice from the mortuary, assured him that they did. He led them out, his torch flickering ahead across the garden.

'Christ,' moaned Bradbury to Woods. 'But what could I do?'

'Not a lot,' sympathized the constable.

'Tell the station we want some help anyway. And make sure nobody slopes off before we've got their names and addresses.'

'Right,' said Woods, and went out to use the radio in the car.

Martyn, who also felt that things were well beyond his control or influence, went back to the billiards-room to see if George wanted a drink, or simply company.

'I'll have a brandy,' he said. He seemed recovered from his earlier shock and managed a weak smile when Martyn explained to him what all the noise was about.

The search took about half an hour, eventually involving even Martyn and George. George, at Bradbury's request, led them down into the cellars, and Martyn joined the outdoor group to show them the outbuildings. A dead rat was discovered at the back of the old stables, shortly after which the battery in Rob's torch expired and there was a hiatus as they waited for another to be found. A cluster of bats fluttered amongst them in the darkness, causing a short-lived panic. The tall girl in white ran into a bunch of nettles but insisted on continuing despite the discomfort.

Indoors, Lawrence Cutt's team grew dusty in the top floor rooms, then swept through the first floor bedrooms and from there disappeared down into the cellars, where they grew even dustier. But nowhere, neither inside nor out, was there the slightest sign of Elaine Webster or, for that matter, any evidence that she had ever been there.

Another four policemen arrived, this time in uniform, and quickly went over the whole house and grounds again but with no more success than the amateurs had enjoyed. Elaine, had she ever been there, had vanished as completely as on the Friday night.

The only positive outcome of all this activity was to re-launch the party into its second phase. Everyone congregated in and around the kitchen, needing a drink and feeling that they had earned one after their efforts. Even the policemen accepted a glass of beer. There was an air of excitement and a faint taste of danger and the unknown that had already established that this party would be remembered for years to come. The few guests who had to leave did so reluctantly. The vast majority stayed on to talk over the night's events.

The old story of the ghost – the woman in grey who haunted the top floor – had been revived by someone and Rob loudly confessed that he and Martyn had already considered the possibility that Martyn's sighting of Elaine on the Friday night had been indeed just such a ghost.

'But how could it be?' someone asked. 'She isn't dead!'

'Don't know, do we?' said someone else.

'How could a ghost place a block of ice in a car?'

'Why ever not? Ghosts have been known to do all kinds of things!'

The house echoed with opinions and speculation.

The policemen had gathered for a quiet smoke on the steps at the front of the house.

'Just take everyone's name,' instructed Bradbury. 'There's nothing else we can do tonight. And take all these car numbers while you're at it.'

Constable Woods moved slowly to do this. The four uniformed men, whose help was no longer needed, put their hats back on, got in their car and drove away.

Martyn, still keeping George company in the seclusion of the old billiards-room, noticed that he had perked up somewhat. No doubt he was relieved that Elaine had not been discovered and that he had not had to confront her. Nevertheless his next statement was something of a surprise.

'There are some fireworks,' he said.

'Pardon?' said Martyn.

'There are some fireworks,' repeated George, 'that I got for the party. They're in that top sideboard drawer.'

'Oh,' said Martyn, not sure what he could be suggesting. Surely not that they might still set them off?

But apparently so. 'Come on then,' said George, standing. 'No point in wasting them.'

'Are you sure that you want to?' protested Martyn.

'What, to set them off? Yes. Why ever not?' And he left the room, so Martyn had to follow.

Viewed dispassionately as a fireworks display, what followed might not have been much to write home about. Coming when it did, after a night of festivity and attempted murder, it seemed a magnificent, defiant gesture that brought everyone whooping out onto the lawn.

George set them up and Martyn, armed with a box of borrowed matches, set them off. There were Roman Candles, Volcanoes and Diamond Cascades. Bottles were found for the half-dozen rockets that left a starry trail above the house and then exploded into tiny, transient galaxies. There was a Catherine Wheel that went fitfully round until the nail that was holding it fell out and it ended its life writhing in the grass.

Each new shower of sparks and stars brought a ragged cheer. Although the sky was now pitch black above them, it was still warm – warm enough for most of the men to have long since discarded their jackets and turned back the cuffs of their shirts. The dress of the women, too, had lost its initial smartness so that the whole bunch of them now had the appearance – as the light from a Roman Candle illuminated them – of revellers who had stood the course and taken some knocks on the way.

Martyn had just placed a match to the touch-paper of the last and biggest of the Shooting Stars as an ambulance came through the gates. The driver looked in surprise at the crowd before him and stopped. Stopped, in fact, very close to the Shooting Star, which was now fizzing prior to the moment when it would commence lobbing balls of light into the air. The first of its dull explosions startled the ambulancemen; the white light that burned for a few seconds above them revealed them opening the back doors of the ambulance and glancing skywards in surprise. The second stage explosion showed them with the doors open. And the third illuminated Josie clambering down out of the ambulance, with her green hair, her party frock and one leg clad up to the knee in a white plaster cast.

Her appearance, as a sort of unscheduled queen of the fireworks, brought a hearty round of cheering and applause to which she responded by raising her arms in the manner of a triumphant boxer. George and Martyn both went forward to meet her and ask her how she was.

'Oh, all right,' she said. 'The sods wanted to keep me in but I

168

said no chance!'

The ambulancemen, unnerved by their reception, had got back in their ambulance and were manoeuvring to get out of the gates again.

Josie's return had, by common consent, brought the fireworks display to an end. People began to drift back indoors. A few sadly admitted that they would have to be leaving. Martyn helped Josie up the steps and inside the house.

'Now,' he said solicitously, 'can I get you anything?'

'Bacardi and Coke,' she said.

'All right,' he laughed, sat her down and went to fetch her one.

Rob, he noticed in passing, had gone to sleep at the foot of the staircase. Samantha was disappearing outside hand-in-hand with one of the Harlequin men.

Josie, understandably, wanted to know all about the accident and what had happened after it. She knew about the cow and the narrowness of their escape; these were things that they had been able to tell her at the hospital. But she did not know the reactions of the police, the speculation about Elaine's involvement and the enthusiastic search of the house.

'Sounds great,' she said. 'Trust me to miss out on all the fun.'

'Awful for George though,' said Martyn.

'Oh, I don't know. He looks all right.'

And, indeed, George did seem to have got over his earlier shock. He was talking, happily enough by the looks of it, with Kevin and Maurice, his two workmates at the mortuary. They were presumably talking shop, though exactly what that would entail Martyn was not eager to discover. Anyway, George had a glass in his hand and the colour had returned to his face.

'So what's going to happen now?' asked Josie, finishing her drink and handing Martyn her empty glass for a refill.

'I don't know. Nothing much I don't suppose. I think they've given up for tonight.'

'So we'll have the fuzz up here again tomorrow?'

'I should think so, yes.'

In fact, Detective Sergeant Bradbury and Detective Constable Woods were just interrupting George's conversation with Maurice

169

and Kevin to inform him that they were leaving and that, as Martyn had surmised, they would be returning to continue their investigations the following morning. George walked with them to the door and stood to watch them go.

'Cheers,' said Josie, as Martyn brought in another Bacardi. 'Do you want to write something on my leg?'

Martyn took a felt-tipped pen from the bureau and wrote, 'To a girl who deserves a break. Love. Martyn,' on her cast. Josie laughed.

It was well after midnight and into the small hours of the morning before the guests started to depart in any numbers. No-one really wanted to admit that the party was over. There had been high drama, action, excitement, police, an ambulance, fireworks and tons of booze. It had been like something from the movies.

'The best birthday party of all time!' called out Lawrence Cutt as he got into his Granada estate. Like everyone else he had drunk more than he should and was followed by cries of 'Drive carefully!' that were only half-joking as he drove away through the gates.

Slowly the drive emptied of cars and the house, although still lit from top to bottom, fell silent. Rob was prodded into wakefulness by the end of his wife's shoe and off they went, with her driving. Almost everybody else had already gone, saying good night to George who had stationed himself outside the front door somewhat like a vicar after his Sunday morning service. The women kissed him and most of the men shook his hand. It was all out of a mixture of gratitude for the good time that he had given them and admiration that he had done it in the face of what was now generally accepted as his wife's attempt to kill him.

By two-thirty a.m. there were only four people left at the White House and one of those was on the point of leaving. It was Mr Charlesworth, and George, Martyn and Josie had come out to see him off.

'Well, well, well,' said Mr Charlesworth, 'I seem to be the last.'

'Very glad you could come,' said George.

'Are you all right now, young man?' asked Mr Charlesworth, turning to Martyn.

'Yes, thanks.' To tell the truth, he felt exhausted. He had only stayed up in case George needed a hand with anything once the party was over.

'It was a near thing though by the sound of it,' went on Mr Charlesworth, seemingly as unwilling as anybody else had been to climb into his car and leave. 'I'm just thankful that neither yourself nor your young lady will be coming before me on the slab tomorrow.'

This made Martyn shiver slightly. He could have done without the reminder of how close he had come to a violent death. But Josie seemed not to have heard. She was staring out, across to where the town lay below them, the pattern of its street lights presenting an illuminated map of itself.

'What's going on over there?' she said, puzzled.

The other three moved forward to look. She pointed and they saw what she had seen: a small group of tiny pin-pricks of light, too random to be car headlights and, anyway, outside the town itself on its eastern edge.

'It's the cemetery,' said George. 'Isn't it?'

'Oh yes,' said Mr Charlesworth. 'What can they be up to?' Then, with a click of his fingers, he remembered. 'It'll be that exhumation! Of course. A pound to a penny that's what it is!'

'What's that?' asked Josie.

'Well, it's Carter who's dealing with it, not me. But it's caused a bit of a fuss. Don't get one of them every day. Or every night for that matter.'

'But what is it?' insisted Josie.

'It's where they dig up somebody who's already been buried, isn't it?' said Martyn helpfully. Then gave way to a yawn that he had been fighting to suppress. 'Oh, sorry.'

'Yes,' said Mr Charlesworth. 'One of our customers. A lady that we did a P.M. on a few weeks ago. Or rather Carter did. Like I say, it's not one of mine. But you might remember her, George. Anyway, apparently one of her relatives has gone and complained to the police that she'd been poisoned. P.M. showed nothing of the sort but the police think there might be something in it so they've been to the coroner and he's ordered that they dig her up and have another look.'

171

'Sounds horrible,' said Josie.

'Well, yes. That's why they always do it at night. There'll be a real little gang of them down there. Pathologist, coroner, police inspector. And half-a-dozen constables with shovels in their hands. Anyway, must get off.'

'Do we know who?' asked George softly.

'Who what?' said Mr Charlesworth, halfway into his car.

George had put a hand upon the bonnet, as much it seemed for support as to delay Mr Charlesworth's departure.

'Do we know the name of the deceased? The one they're exhuming?

'Yes, I was told. It's a woman. A Mrs, er . . . Mac something or other. . . .'

'Mackay,' said George quietly.

'Mackay!' echoed Mr Charlesworth. 'That's it!'

He slammed the car door shut and wound down the window. 'Good night then,' he called, and pulled away.

Martyn, Josie and George remained where they were for a moment without speaking, each still mesmerized by the tiny group of distant lights and the gruesomeness of the task that they now knew them to indicate. Mr Charlesworth's car went away below them down the hill.

CHAPTER TWENTY-ONE

Martyn and Josie went off to their separate beds, leaving the wreckage of the party behind them.

George Webster did not. He stood in the lounge, poured himself a large whisky and contemplated the wreckage of his life.

It was less than six weeks sin⌣e he had murdered Elaine. He had done so from the simplest of motives: revenge, and a wish to be rid of the woman to whom he had given everything and who, in return, had held him in such contempt that she had not only insulted and belittled him but had not even sought to hide her infidelities from him. It had been her total indifference that had weighed more heavily than her sexual betrayal. It had been a crime not of passion but of desperation; one committed in very cold blood indeed.

His greatest asset as a murderer had been his familiarity with death. It meant that he had neither over-estimated it nor been panicked by it. He had not expected the Heavens to open and a Divine voice to cry for vengeance. His job had taught him that death was a common, everyday event, one for which the State had an elaborate machinery. Being himself an important part of it, he knew that machinery well. Knew how to throw a spanner in it.

Thus he had achieved the perfect murder. Or so he had believed at the time. The world had been conned into thinking that Elaine had taken his money and left him when, all the time, her body, in fourteen separate parts, had been buried with all due ceremony. In fact, overall, with a great deal more ceremony than most bodies could ever hope for.

It had been done, finished, got away with. The police had confirmed that themselves in trying to stick Elaine's identity on a

173

drowned body in Devon. Convinced that he was beyond suspicion, George had celebrated by going to the Friar Tuck to persuade Josie to come and be his housekeeper. She was to have been the cornerstone of his new life.

The problems had begun with the arrival of Martyn Culley, this tall, polite young man with a southern accent who was, moreover, intelligent, university-educated and well-spoken. His appearance had perhaps been slightly unkempt – jeans, tee-shirt, training-shoes – but his manner had been respectful and his character had displayed a straightforwardness and honesty that amounted almost to innocence.

Yet what he had come to tell George had been palpably impossible.

'It's about your wife,' he had said. 'It's just that I think I saw her and talked to her something over a week ago. I think she was a lady who stopped and gave me a lift when I was hitch-hiking to London.'

And, when questioned about the date on which this had happened, he had been adamant: May fifth. By which date, as a matter of indisputable fact, Elaine had been a week dead. She had been cut up and stored in black plastic bags, two of which had already been buried, another three cremated. So, whatever she had been doing on May fifth, it had not been giving Martyn Culley a lift along the M4.

Culley's visit had left George in a desperate dilemma. Was this just some kind of absurd mistake? Or was there some more sinister purpose behind it? Blackmail for example? George was known to have money. His unexpected legacy had been well-publicized in the local press. Had Culley in some way discovered the truth about Elaine's death and was he now coming to George with this strange tale as an oblique approach to blackmailing him?

Not certain what to do for the best, George had let him go but had asked him for a phone number where he could be contacted. After a day of agonized thought, he had decided that to do nothing was too much of a risk. He could not just leave Culley alone to see what his next step might be. He had to contact him again, observe him, find out why the hell he had turned up on his doorstep with this pack of lies.

It worried him particularly that Culley could give little reason for being in Arncaster. 'I'm just here visiting friends,' he had said, which was too much of a coincidence to swallow. That he should, on his way to London, have been given a lift by a woman coming from Arncaster – whoever she was – and then turn up himself in Arncaster a week later, just in time to be able to read about Elaine's disappearance in the local press and come rushing up to the White House to tell his story: such a situation could not be produced by the workings of blind chance.

(On this point George was right. Martyn Culley had not turned up in Arncaster owing to the workings of blind chance. His visit had been prompted by a brief love affair with a woman who had told him that she lived there. This was not, however, an explanation that he could offer to the woman's husband; hence George had been left to his own suspicions.)

On the defensive and prepared to take drastic action if need be, George had invited Culley to become gardener and general factotum at the house.

And Culley had accepted. Perhaps he too welcomed this arrangement by which he could stay in close contact with George and was planning to use it for his own purposes. It had now become a game of cat-and-mouse, though with George still uncertain in which role he himself was cast.

There had inevitably been complications with Josie. It had been obvious that she fancied Culley from the first time that the young man had crossed the threshold, and George had resigned himself to the probability that they would be copulating like rabbits the moment his back was turned. There was nothing he could do about it. He could never have competed with this tall, handsome youth; could probably never have got anywhere with Josie himself anyway, even had Culley not appeared on the scene. That was all suddenly beside the point. The threat of exposure as a murderer had made him abandon any designs he had been harbouring on Josie's shapely little body.

So Culley had come to the house and George had watched and waited. Not that he needed to do so for very long. On his first evening there Culley had embarked on a conversation that had

175

come near to confirming George's worst fears.

Culley had said something like, 'Does having to deal with dead bodies all the time affect your attitude towards living people?'

George, suspicious and on the lookout for the slightest hint that Culley might know more than he was letting on, had not answered.

And Culley had insisted: 'Does it make you think any less of human life?'

This had thrown George into a small panic. He had snapped back rudely and left the room, fearful of what more explicit reference to Elaine's murder Culley might be about to make next. But he seemed to have decided to play a waiting game and, when they had met at breakfast the following morning, all had been sweetness and light.

Another such worrying conversation had come a few evenings later. They had all been drinking at the end of one of those warm spring days with which they had recently been blessed and this time it had been Josie, reeling about the place and pouring Bacardi and Coke over herself, who had suddenly announced, 'We know things, George. We know things.'

Culley, George had noticed, had been discomfited and tried to stop her, but she had gone on: 'We can stop you ever selling this house, George. We can stop you doing anything we want.'

It was a clear threat that could no longer be ignored. Obviously Culley had confided in her; they were now in it together; all set to take him for every penny he had, or to play him along for as long as it amused them before going to the police.

Although George had resigned himself to their conducting their sexual relationship under his roof, his awareness of their intimacy increased his feeling that he was being conspired against. In any confrontation he would be outnumbered two to one.

(It had, of course, never occurred to him that Josie's threat was simply that she knew about the ghost that was said to haunt the upper storey. His career as a mortician had hardened him against all ideas of life after death. He had heard about the supposed ghost shortly after he had bought the house and been amused by it.)

There was only one solution. The same solution that he had used to silence Elaine. His success in killing her had encouraged him

176

into thinking that what he had done once he could do again – only this time killing two birds with one stone.

He had planned carefully. He could not, he knew, repeat the formula he had used for Elaine. Simultaneously to feed sleeping tablets to two of them, to suffocate them both with carbon monoxide, to dissect both bodies and then be faced with the risk of disposing of twice the number of black plastic bags seemed not just to double the odds against possible success but to multiply them a hundredfold. It would have to be by a completely different method.

It had come to him one afternoon while in the mortuary.

'That ice-machine needs adjusting,' Maurice had complained 'Temperature's too low. You can't get the ice out.'

They had an ice-making machine at the hospital which churned out ice-cubes, used mainly to suppress haemorrhaging, but which the mortuary staff often utilized when specimens had to be packed with ice to keep them at a low temperature.

George was never conscious of the mental leap by which the picture of a lump of ice became associated with the spiralling downhill run from the White House but there, suddenly, was his plan. Certainly the danger of the downhill drive had been something he had long been aware of: Elaine had once had a slight bump taking it too fast after dark. But there it was: he would pack the brake pedal with a lump of ice.

One slight problem was that the big Volvo was far from ideal for his plan. Its makers' boasts about its safety might well prove all too true. He exchanged it that same day for a sports car, one that would encourage speeding and leave its occupants more vulnerable.

The idea of the birthday party was the final part of his plan and was his insurance against things going wrong. He could have blocked up the brake pedal at any time, then invited Martyn and Josie to take a ride in the car. But had something gone wrong and the ice been discovered, then everything would have pointed back to himself as being the only possible culprit.

Holding an extravagant birthday party was the simplest way of ensuring that, in the event of a cock-up, there would be fifty or more possible suspects. And, since it would be his car that had been tampered with, he would be the least likely.

177

(Even then he would probably have aborted the whole thing had he known of Martyn's plans to leave within a week. But he did not. Martyn, nervous of Josie's reaction, had kept his thoughts on leaving to himself.)

George had another whisky and lit a cigarette. He was still dizzy and sick after the long evening of the party during which his fortunes had soared, fallen, then soared again; till finally falling to their lowest ebb.

To start with, everything had gone like a dream. The party had taken off, his guests becoming so preoccupied with one another that they gave little thought to their host or what he might be up to. He had stage-managed the car-parking so that his own car had stayed well clear of those of his guests, standing just inside the gates with uninterrupted access to the road ahead.

He had earlier estimated the size of the ice-block that he would need, had filled a suitable tupperware box with water and placed it in the large freezer at the back of the garage. Then, at an appropriate moment and under cover of dusk, he had taken it out, pushed it from its mould and jammed it tightly under the Triumph's brake pedal. It had been a perfect fit.

Even more perfect had been Martyn's eagerness to drive into town and to take Josie with him.

'We seem to be running out of mixers,' George had said. 'Can you look after things while I dash over to that off-licence in Ballantyne Street?'

The response had been exactly the one that he had been counting on. 'Look, I'll go. I'd much rather do that than stay here in charge of this lot!'

After that things had gone badly wrong. Martyn had returned intact and in a police car. The ice had not melted away as it should have done but had been discovered, though George was glad to see that Detective Sergeant Bradbury did not seem over-impressed by it as a piece of evidence. Nevertheless, he had felt himself cornered. Culley, despite his show of innocence, might well have guessed who had tried to kill him and why. Even if George had got away with it as far as the police were concerned, who knew what steps Culley might now take? To say nothing of his little tart. If

178

they both knew about Elaine's murder and had just escaped from a murder attempt themselves, it would surely not take them long to put two and two together.

But then had come the most amazing turn-about of all.

The Detective Sergeant had been questioning George and Martyn Culley in the old billiards-room, Culley had gone out to get a drink, there had been some noisy shouting from the hall and Culley had come back in the company of the other policeman, Detective Constable Woods.

'What's the matter?' the Detective-Sergeant had said.

'This man', said Woods, 'says that he [Culley] saw this man's wife [Elaine] in this house on Friday night.'

This had taken a moment to sink in, but, once it did, it was as if a conjuror had waved a magic wand, an impenetrable veil had been lifted and suddenly all was crystal clear.

George had questioned Culley himself just to be sure.

'The woman that you saw in this house on Friday night. . . .'

'Yes?'

'She was the same one you gave a lift to in London?'

'Yes.'

This had clinched it.

Martyn Culley was not out to blackmail him or to expose him to the police. He had never met Elaine Webster, not on May fifth or at any other time. But he was honest in his belief that he had. He believed it because he had, in fact, met Margaret, Elaine's sister. It was Margaret who had given him a lift, just as it was Margaret who had come to Arncaster on the Friday and visited the White House.

(George could not have known about the poor photocopy of the photograph of Elaine which Samantha had acquired and on the basis of which Martyn had been confirmed in his mistake. Certainly the two sisters were sufficiently alike to be confused one for the other when seen in fuzzy reproduction.)

Margaret, Elaine Webster's sister, had visited Arncaster on the previous Friday by arrangement with George. He had suggested to her that she might like to take possession of the clothes and other personal effects that Elaine had left behind her. They were of no use to him and he would be glad to see the back of them, whereas

179

Margaret, being of similar build and only a year older than her sister, could make good use of them.

She had come to Arncaster by train, then taken a taxi to the mortuary where George was working.

'Have you heard from her at all?' she asked him.

'No,' he said flatly.

'No, neither have I. I can't think where the hell she can have gone to. Have you been to the police?'

'Yes.'

There was a faint antagonism and distrust between them. He could see that she held him responsible for the breakdown of his marriage. And, after all, why not? Seen from afar, he was the older man who had taken her sister off and then made her unhappy.

He had given Margaret a key to the White House and she had got back in her taxi.

He had neglected to explain to her about the presence of either Martyn Culley or Josie in the house since they had conveniently taken themselves off to Blackpool that same morning and were intending to stay overnight. Margaret would not meet them; there was, therefore, no reason that she should be told about them.

Then, for some reason that George had never had explained to him (their row after Martyn's announcement that he would be leaving), Culley and the girl had cut short their Blackpool trip and returned late that afternoon and, evidently, had seen Margaret. Just as Margaret evidently had seen them.

What George could still not understand was why this chance meeting should never have been mentioned to him by anyone. He himself had come across Margaret hurrying down the hill away from the White House. He had turned his car round and given her a lift to the station. She had seemed agitated and been unwilling to talk; but he had not questioned her, thinking only that she was still resentful of him. Odd, though, that she had not mentioned seeing Culley. Had she or had she not recognized him as the same young man to whom she had given the lift?

(She had, of course, recognized him instantly, and been petrified. She had been foolish enough to have seduced a young hitch-hiker and had cursed herself for it afterwards. But why should he now turn up in her brother-in-law's house 200 miles north? Fortunately he had seemed as dismayed as she was and, while his attention had been distracted, she had made her escape by the back stairs.)

George's understanding of what had happened still had many gaps in it. Why Culley had got the wrong end of the stick and believed that Margaret was Elaine he could not begin to guess. Perhaps it had been some kind of obscure joke on her part. If so, it had had near-disastrous consequences.

(In fact, Margaret had borrowed her sister's identity for much the same reason that she had lied about her name. It was to distance herself from the events of that afternoon, of which she was mildly ashamed. She had taken the name Janet Megson at random and then, when her conversation with Martyn had demanded that she provide a background for this character, she had saved herself the trouble of inventing one by borrowing one ready-made, the first that came into her head – that of her sister.)

But never mind the details; never mind that there were still odd gaps in the story as far as George was concerned. What mattered was that he could now see that Culley had made a genuine mistake and certainly knew nothing about how the real Elaine had met her sticky end. At the same time, everyone had jumped to the conclusion that it was Elaine herself who had returned and placed the ice beneath the brake pedal and that it was he, George, who was the intended victim!

A miracle indeed. He was not only free from suspicion of making the attempt on Culley's life and immensely relieved to know that Culley and his girl-friend were no threat at all, but he was also receiving sympathetic treatment as the man whose wife had returned to kill him.

It would certainly have been his second perfect murder had it succeeded. One for which the main suspect would have been the victim of his first! Not that George regretted the failure any longer. He had wanted Culley and his girl-friend dead only because they had seemed to threaten him with exposure. Now, knowing that everything had sprung from the Elaine/Margaret mix-up, he wished them dead no longer.

That had been – how long ago? three, four hours earlier – when everything seemed to have been sorting itself out for the best. Relieved and exhilarated, George had proposed the fireworks display. It had seemed a fitting celebration of his escape.

Now, as the first glimpse of dawn appeared on the edge of the night sky, such celebration seemed premature indeed. George went to pour himself another whisky and found the bottle empty. He had drunk most of it but to little effect. He felt cold, alone and helpless. The new day that was arriving brought with it his inevitable downfall.

Inevitable from the moment that Josie had spotted the tiny lights in the cemetery and Mr Charlesworth had said, 'It'll be that exhumation! Of course. A pound to a penny that's what it is!'

It was the exhumation that now threatened him. Having escaped scot free from his second attempt at murder, he was suddenly faced with the exposure of his first.

For the coffin that had been dug up during the night and that would be standing in the mortuary awaiting the ministrations of the pathologist first thing that morning contained not only the mortal remains of Mrs McKay but also part of the mortal remains of Elaine Webster.

Which part exactly George could not say. But did it matter? The discovery that there was part of another body in the coffin – a part that had been skilfully dissected and wrapped in a plastic bag not unlike those regularly used in the mortuary – would surely cause an investigation to be launched that would sooner or later land up on George's own doorstep. It was known that his wife had disappeared and it was known when. It was also known when Mrs McKay had been buried. Though George, more than most, was well aware of the fallibility of the police, he could not hope that they would fail to see the possible connection. And then the cat would be well and truly out of the bag.

He could see only one chance of escape – it was desperate, but no more than he himself was – and that was if he went to the mortuary there and then and removed the incriminating evidence from the coffin before Mr Collins got to it. He might already be too late. Exhumations were so rare for there to be no routine approach to one. It might well be that Mr Collins had gone ahead and performed his post mortem that night without the assistance of a mortician. The remains of Elaine might have been discovered already.

Still, that was a chance he would have to take. It was the only one he had. Taking the mortuary keys from the hall table drawer, he crept from the silent house, confident at least that neither Martyn nor Josie were likely to be stirring. He would have to drive Elaine's green Mini. His own car was, of course, well out of commission.

For a moment he feared that the Mini would refuse to start. Its weeks of inactivity had made the motor reluctant to fire. He was sweating and cursing the ludicrous irony of Elaine's own car frustrating him at this juncture, when it finally coughed into life. He drove out of the gates and down the hill.

The first flush of dawn was beginning to climb higher and a chorus of bird song came to him through his open window. The town was still deserted, so that he felt safe in driving straight through a set of traffic lights that turned red as he approached, following his familiar route to the hospital.

Arriving, he saw immediately that there were no cars outside the mortuary. He gave a gasp of relief, stopped outside the door and hurried to open it.

At first he could not understand why the key refused to turn. It was, he checked, the right key: why, he wondered as he desperately jabbed it back into the lock, should it not work now as it had worked on every other morning?

Till he realized that the door was already unlocked. His heart fell. There must be someone inside already. Perhaps Mr Collins, perhaps anyone. Anyone at all would dash even the faint hope that he retained. Or was it just possible that they had delivered the coffin and then, sleepy and wanting to be away, had omitted to lock the door behind them?

He had to take any chance he could. He gingerly opened the door, stepped inside and closed it behind him.

There were no lights, no sounds of activity. Trying to control his excited breathing, he stepped cautiously forward. Pushed open the other door which led to the laying-out room with its rows of

183

refrigerated drawers.

'Hello?'

His heart stopped as a voice came from nowhere. Then a patch of darkness detached itself from the wall and moved towards him.

'Oh, Mr Webster, isn't it?'

It was a policeman, one whom George knew by sight, who had last visited the mortuary as accident officer in a case where a school-teacher had driven his car into a lamppost.

George opened his mouth to reply but no sound came. He tried again. 'Yes . . . yes.'

'Only nobody told me you'd be coming.'

George, recovering from the shock, noticed the coffin, still with some sods of earth attached, standing on a trolley in the far corner. Whether it had already been opened and the lid replaced it was impossible to say.

Was there a way, any way, of getting rid of the policeman?

'You're, er . . . you're on guard duty are you?' he asked in a voice he barely recognized as his own.

'I am.' The constable seemed tired and bored. 'Got the short straw didn't I. Everybody else is home in their beds and here I am guarding a corpse.'

George's hopes rose a notch or two. 'I see. Everybody else gone then, have they?'

'Well, the lads that dug her up, yes. But not the Chief Inspector and the Coroner and all. They've gone back to the station. There's been a right to-do.'

This put pay to George's brief spurt of optimism.

'Why?' he asked fearfully. 'What's happened?'

'Oh, I don't know. They pulled me in off the beat to stand here till they got back. But something ain't as it should be, that's for sure. They're all running around like blue-arsed flies.'

'Really,' said George.

He felt himself overwhelmed by a rush of despair, acquiescing in the resolution that Fate clearly intended for him, with just a residue of relief that it was at last over. Knowing the worst at least meant that there was nothing worse to be feared.

'You all right, sir?' said the constable, peering at him through

184

the gloom.

'Yes,' murmured George. 'I've, er, . . . I've just something I want to collect.'

And he gave a weak smile, turned and shuffled away to the dissecting room.

'Good night then,' called the constable after him.

In fact it was morning. Even in the short time that George had spent inside the mortuary, the day had taken a stride forward, so he drove back under a lightening sky that promised another day of sunshine. The birds were now in full voice; a rabbit scuttled across the road in front of his car as he started the climb back up to the White House.

It was a mockery of everything he felt, all this stirring and promise. His own future promised only public exposure and condemnation as his past, released from Mrs McKay's coffin, rushed to overtake it.

He parked the Mini in its exact same spot and went into the house. At least the police had not got there before him. They were still, no doubt, puzzling over what they had found and were taking time to convince themselves of the truth of it. When they finally did so, they would be after him soon enough.

In fact it was Josie who found him.

It was two hours later. She had been awakened by a nagging pain in her broken foot and, anyway, needed a pee. She had swung herself out of bed and thumped painfully along the corridor to the bathroom.

George was lying in the bath, his head back and resting on a pillow. The water that half-covered him was red with his own blood that had run copiously, encouraged by the alcohol and the warmth, from the incisions made in each wrist. He had cut hard and straight just below the heel of the hand, using the scalpel that he had borrowed from the dissecting room.

Josie's eyes widened. She gave a gulp of nausea, then screamed. She was still screaming when Martyn came running to find out what was going on.

CHAPTER TWENTY-TWO

The funeral was a week later, by which time the weather had broken and it was raining steadily, making treacherous the grassy slopes of the cemetery. The few mourners moved cautiously to gather around the open grave, keeping their heads down, out of respect and out of the rain, as George's coffin was lowered.

Elaine had not turned up, nor had anyone from her family. There was Martyn, Josie – still with her plaster cast on – Kevin and Maurice from the mortuary, a couple of distant relatives, and a few friends and colleagues, including Mr Charlesworth.

Nothing like the number that had come to the party, observed Martyn with an uncharacteristic touch of bitterness.

George's grave was only five along from that of Mrs McKay, where the disturbed earth and a corner chipped off the headstone testified to the exhumation that she had undergone. And pointlessly at that, for no sooner had she been so rudely disturbed than a message had arrived from the police station to stop everything: the accusations had been withdrawn. The relative who had alleged poison had broken down and admitted that the whole thing was a malicious invention; one that the relative had not really expected to be believed or to have had such drastic consequences as Mrs McKay's disinterment.

The instructions were that the coffin be returned, unopened, to the grave, but the Coroner, nervous about the legal situation of reversing an order which he himself had issued, ordered instead that the coffin be kept in the mortuary until he had had time to consider things further. In the event, the coffin, guarded by a police officer, stood waiting for two days while the legal arguments

186

raged and precedents were sought. Finally the Home Office instructed that the coffin be returned, unopened, to its resting place.

With that little matter off his mind, the Coroner was free to conduct an inquest on George Webster. Mr Charlesworth, who had carried out the post mortem, submitted his report. The police constable who had been guarding the coffin and been the last person to see George Webster alive testified to his nervous and exhausted condition. And Detective Sergeant Bradbury told the story of the motor accident brought about by the block of ice and the speculation that there had been to the effect that Elaine Webster had been trying to kill her husband.

It was with a sympathetic expression that the Coroner pronounced his verdict: suicide.

And he had something else to say: 'It does seem to me clear that the deceased took his own life for one reason and one reason only. That is, that he had become depressed and upset by what had happened that night. And, in particular, by what it seems might well have been his wife's returning secretly to the house and making a vicious and cunning attempt on his life. It is a sad irony that a night that had begun so happily – with a birthday party – should have ended so tragically. The court trusts that the police are actively investigating these events.'

To show that they were, the police issued a statement saying that they wished to interview Elaine Webster, who they believed could help them with their enquiries, and asking anyone who knew of her whereabouts to contact them.

And so George was laid to rest in a hurried ceremony in the rain. There was to be no meal or gathering afterwards since no-one knew who should have arranged it.

'Poor old chap,' muttered Josie to Martyn as they moved away from the graveside.

'He never seemed very happy, did he,' agreed Martyn.

He still, truth to tell, found it difficult to reconcile what he remembered of Elaine Webster and their afternoon of love together with the fact that she would soon afterwards have been attempting to murder her amiable, well-meaning husband. It was a funny world, reflected Martyn, one in which not everybody was what they seemed.

He was leaving the White House, as Josie knew and had now accepted. In fact, he had stayed on as long as he had only for the inquest and funeral. Then, two days ago, Rob had called up at the house with a letter for him.

'Oh great,' exclaimed Martyn on opening it.

'What is it?'

'Answer to a job application I made. Theatre administration. They want me to go for an interview.'

'Oh, well done,' said Rob. 'Must have a drink to celebrate.'

It was unlikely, as Martyn knew from long experience, that the interview would lead to an actual job, but it did give him a new purpose in life. And, since the interviews were being conducted in London, it got him out of the White House and back on his travels.

Josie hobbled to the front gateway to see him off.

'I'm not going to cry,' she said, ''cause I know you'll come and see me again, won't you?'

'Of course I will,' he said and meant it. He had developed a real fondness for her and had every intention of keeping in touch.

They kissed, he promised that he would ring as soon as he got to London and, bag in hand, went jogging off down the hill.

'Bye love,' she called after him and went back, misty-eyed, into the house. She had learned early on that nothing in this life was forever but wondered why some things could not sometimes last just a bit longer than they did.

Even her job at the house would end as soon as the property was sold. The solicitor handling everything had told her that she could stay on till then and prepare everything inside the house for auction. So that her immediate prospects were of weeks of cleaning and sorting and then eviction.

She had done nothing until Martyn had gone and now, wanting to occupy herself, made a casual sort of start by emptying the sideboard in the lounge. There were some pieces of silver, some of them silver-plated. All needed polishing. She started on a sugar bowl, then picked up a coffee-pot, which felt heavy, as though it had something in it.

She opened the top, turned it upside down and shook it.

A small torrent of banknotes, fastened into little bundles, came out. They filled her lap, then spilled over onto the floor and around her feet.

If you have enjoyed this book and would like to receive details of other Walker Adventure titles, please write to:

Adventure Editor
Walker and Company
720 Fifth Avenue
New York, NY 10019